Life in His Body

*A Simple Guide
to Active Cell Life*

David L. Finnell

Touch Pub
Hous

D1472891

© 1995 by David L. Finnell
Published by TOUCH Outreach Ministries
P.O. Box 19888 Houston, TX 77079
800-735-5865

Also available from:
TOUCH Resource
3, Marine Parade Central
Singapore 1544
(65) 440-7544

ISBN: 1-880828-87-1

FOR A FREE CATALOG OF
TOUCH PUBLICATIONS BOOKS AND MATERIALS,
PLEASE CALL
1-800-735-5865 (USA)
713-497-7901 (INTERNATIONAL)

Dedication

To Linda, my wife, and my sons, Shane and Nathan

For all they have endured,
for their faithfulness,
for their unfailing love.

Table of Contents

Foreword

While this may be your first exposure to what God is doing through the cell church, rest assured that thousands of churches around the world, and hundreds in the U.S.A., are presently moving into this New Testament model! These churches are following in the footsteps of nation impacting churches such as Yoido Full Gospel Church in Korea, Faith Community Baptist Church in Singapore, and Eglise Protestante Baptiste Oeuvres et Mission in the Ivory Coast. As you read this book, let me give you a few words of advice:

Recognize your innate aversion to change. I remember talking with an elderly deacon who had served in a small rural church for over 50 years. When I commented that he must have seen quite a few new things in his time, his reply was "Yep, and I've been against every one of them!" Be careful not to oppose something just because it is new.

Be willing to consider new ways of being the Church. During the time of the first reformation, many missed out on the new thing that God was doing. I believe that we are in the midst of a second reformation, a reformation that will prepare the Church for the great harvest that is coming. Wouldn't it be terrible to sleep through this second reformation?

Be open to learning from a seasoned follower of Christ. God has used David Finnell to impact lives around this world as a Missionary, Pastor, Seminary Professor, and Friend. His years of experience in church planting and teaching make him the perfect person to write this basic training manual for the cell church.

Finally, support your pastor as he leads your church. Leadership is often a difficult, lonely task, especially during times of change. Rather than looking for all the reasons why this won't work, ask God how you can make this dynamic model for the Church a reality in your fellowship.

The chapters which follow are the product of years of experience in church life, both overseas and in America. They will be a major tool in equipping Christians who become members or leaders of a cell group. If you will let it, this book can revolutionize your definition of the word "church."

Ralph W. Neighbour Jr.
President TOUCH International
Singapore

Acknowledgements

M any of the insights in this book are a result of the ministry of Ralph W. Neighbour Jr. I am extremely grateful for the influence he has had on my ministry.

I would like to acknowledge the ministry of David Yonggi Cho from Seoul, Korea and the time I spent studying the life of the church he pastors.

I would also like to acknowledge the Southern Baptist Foreign Mission Board for allowing me the freedom to experiment with the planting of cell churches in Singapore. Some of the material from this book is adapted from the Care Group Manual, which I wrote for the Baptist Centre for Urban Studies (Singapore) in 1982.

I would like to acknowledge the leaders of First Satellite Baptist Church in Singapore (1983) and Community Baptist Fellowship in Lexington, South Carolina (1994), who walked along side of me in building a vision of cell church ministry.

How to Use
This Book

This book is designed to be used as an information and training tool for cell group members and servants (leaders). Chapters 1-8 are appropriate for both members and servants. Chapters 9 and 10 are primarily for training cell servants, but cell members will also gain insights into cell group life. There are at least five different ways you can use this book:

1. It may be taught in small groups prior to establishing your cell groups. Each participant should read a chapter during the week. During the group meeting, follow the discussion questions at the end of each chapter.

2. The book may be taught in one or two weekend workshops or during a retreat, as long as it is taught in small groups. Don't use the book as a resource for lecturing. Allow 10-12 hours for the study and make sure each participant has a book. It would be preferable for participants to read the book before the workshop or retreat.

3. Another approach is to use this book as a discipling tool (Chapters 1-8) during a new member's class or between an experienced cell group member and a new cell group member. The new member can read a chapter during the week and set aside some time each week with the experienced member for personal discipling.

4. If you have the discipline to keep from turning your cell groups into a training session or Bible study, this book may be used as

a training tool during cell group meetings. If used during the cell meetings, ask cell members to study one chapter each week and discuss them during a portion of the cell group meeting. Expand the length of the meeting by about 30 minutes (for a total of about 2 hours) so as not to detract from the dynamic of the cell group meeting. The additional 30 minutes can be added to the 10 minutes spent in the study of the Word. In total, 50 to 60 minutes of the meeting should be spent in studying the materials in this book. The remaining time should be spent in regular cell group activities. Don't turn your cell group into nothing more than a training session. Following the study, return the cell group to its normal length.

5. The book may also be used for personal study by new cell group members or individuals who are interested in understanding the cell group concept.

Section One

Introduction to the Cell Church

1

The Cell Church Concept

— ❖ —

What Is and Isn't a Cell Church

Many have heard of cell groups and some have even participated in them. But the presence of cell groups do not make a cell church. Some churches add cell groups to the other programs and think they have become a cell church. These traditional program-based churches with cell groups differ from cell churches.

There are inherent problems when the historically traditional church finds itself in a modern urban setting. This style of church was designed for the rural context and has been imported into the cities. Many former traditional churches have made creative adjustments and compensations

Youth

Music

Visitation

Sunday School

Activities

Missions

for this dilemma. One of these creative modifications is the seeker service. A seeker church may have cell groups, but most are still built upon the foundation of the traditional church's "come" structure which attempts to lure seekers to a centrally located church facility.

Many fundamental differences lie between a cell church and a traditional church. The following comparisons of the primary differences between them provides a foundation for moving into cell ministry.

If you come from what you consider a traditional church background, and the following descriptions are not representative of the churches in your past, don't be offended. In the right circumstances, a creative traditional church can reach people for Christ and have a meaningful ministry to many people. God bless you as you continue in your calling.

Traditional	**Cell**
A traditional church is program centered. The church has many activities and gatherings. Programs include youth, music, senior adult, education, missions, activities, visitation, etc.	A cell church is people centered. The focus of the church is to meet the intimate needs of its members and non-Christians.

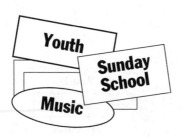

Does this mean the traditional church doesn't care about people? Certainly not. It means the traditional church is organized around programs. Because of this, the program structure, not the lack of compassion of the leadership, limits the ability of the church to meet the intimate needs of many of its members and prospects.

The cell church does have music and youth ministries and some programs. Yet in contrast to the traditional church's basic organizational structure, the cell church is built around people and relationships, not programs.

To illustrate this point, suppose a church discovered that people in their community were hungry. The traditional church would open a soup kitchen to deal with this need and preach to those who came to eat (program to people). The cell church would provide for the same need through the families of a cell group providing meals and other needs to their neighbors as part of building a right to share Christ as the Spirit leads (people to people).

Traditional	**Cell**
A traditional church is building centered. A majority of the programs of the church are located at the church building. The size of the church is limited to the amount of buildings and space a church can afford.	A cell church is community centered. The ministry of the church is decentralized and occurs in the homes and lives of church members and in the community.

The cell church still has buildings, but the focal point of the church is the cell groups. The ministry of the church is decentralized which enables the cell groups in the community to minister more easily to the people where they live. The facilities of a cell church are usually multi-purpose in nature rather than a large expensive sanctuary that is used one or two hours a week. The size of a cell church is not limited by buildings to the degree that a traditional church is limited.

The traditional church is concerned about ministering to people in the community too, but the focal point of the traditional church tends to be the Sunday morning worship service and Sunday School, which meet in the church building along with most of the other programs. As a result, a new traditional church must place a high priority on getting a building.

The traditional church grows like a bee hive. It must provide the space before it can grow. In urban settings where land and buildings are increasingly unaffordable, this places a great financial and spiritual strain upon a growing congregation. The cell church grows like a living organism. The cells multiply and grow, then physical space is provided as space is needed. Since its structure is decentralized, it can more easily adapt to multiple worship services or congregations using rented facilities.

Traditional

A traditional church has a "come" structure. Its outreach to non-Christians is mainly dependent upon bringing people to the church building for Sunday School or services.

Cell

A cell church has a *go structure*. The church is organized to go out to meet and reach non-Christians where they live.

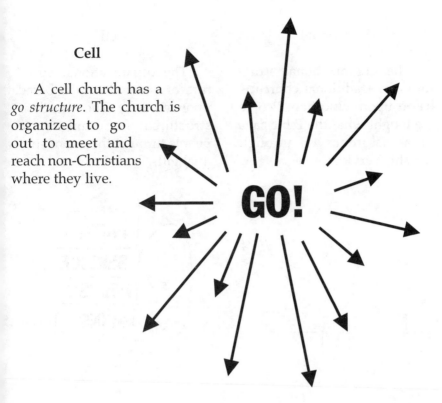

This point refers to what a church is structured or organized to do, not what members may desire to do. Evangelism in the traditional church is designed to take place at the church. Evangelism in the cell church is designed to take place through the cell groups. The cell church may have an evangelistic service at a neutral site away from the church. But an evangelistic service in a cell church is a supportive ministry rather than the norm.

Many traditional churches attempt to reach out into the community, but they do not organize around this objective. A traditional church can have programs in the homes of people, but this would usually be an additional program added to the core of events held at the church building. These added programs can put a tremendous strain on church members who have so many meetings and programs to attend.

Traditional

The organizational structure of a traditional church is based upon education. People are taught what the Bible says in a classroom or through worship services.

Cell

The organizational structure of a cell church is based upon ministry. The church is structured for ministry to people through the use of spiritual gifts.

Are traditional churches unspiritual? No, but here we are talking about structure and organization. The traditional church has a heavy emphasis on Bible learning in classrooms. The cell church teaches the Bible, but there is a stronger emphasis upon learning by *doing* the Word. The church is organized in such a way as to enable people to use their spiritual gifts through the ministry of the cell groups. Mature believers, new believers, and unbelievers come together in someone's home to worship and experience God, minister to one another and lift one another up under the leadership of the Holy Spirit. They pray for one another, and pray for and plan to meet the needs of unbelievers in the community. The traditional church is organized to teach; the cell church is organized to minister.

Traditional

Cell

Traditional church members spend most of their time in activities, programs, and committee meetings at the church. There is little time left to evangelize and minister.

Cell church members have more time to build relationships with and minister to non-Christians.

This has become one of the greatest obstacles to evangelism in the traditional church. Often the schedule of traditional churches is so busy, the most devout members spend most of their non-working hours traveling to and from church and participating in church meetings. Those who are most motivated to do relational evangelism have the least amount of time to do it. Adding cell groups to a traditional church structure only makes matters worse.

The cell church not only provides time for members to spend with non-Christians, it provides accountability to ensure that the members are actually using this time for evangelism. In a pure cell church, the cell groups are not just a part of church life, they are the center of church life. Without accountability, the time provided can be swallowed up in the busyness of urban life.

Traditional

The traditional church is patterned after Western culture. It is a bureaucracy in the sense that it has professional leadership, management, programs, and the desire to maintain things as they are and resist change.

Cell

The cell church is patterned after the New Testament church. Its leadership style is the servant leader (John 13) and every member is a minister. It is task and goal oriented to do whatever it takes to build and expand the kingdom of God.

The priesthood of the believer is foundational to the cell church. The traditional pattern of clergy as professional managers and priests is not compatible with the cell church concept. 1 Peter 2:9 is the pattern for all members to be priests for the purpose of proclaiming Christ. The leadership style in the cell church is that of servant (John 13:12-15; Matthew 23:10-12).

It is extremely difficult to change a traditional church to a cell church because *any* bureaucracy will resist change. If the change is made, it must be understood that a portion of the church will probably leave. (Note: those that leave will soon be replaced.) Another approach might be for a traditional church to sponsor and start a new cell church with a core group (maybe even with the pastor) from the original church. However it is done, it should be done in love with both groups desiring to do whatever it takes to see as many people as possible come to Christ.

Traditional

Most traditional churches use confrontational evangelism and/or invite people to the church building. If people aren't ready to accept Christ, or aren't willing to come to the church building, the traditional church is often limited in its ability to reach them.

Cell

The cell church emphasizes relational evangelism. This involves building relationships with individuals, then after a relationship has been built, cell members present the claims of Christ under the leadership of the Holy Spirit. The non-Christian is brought into the cell groups and/or other ministries which meet in member's homes.

There is nothing wrong with confronting people with the gospel. When people are ready, they should be confronted. But, confronting strangers who are not ready for confrontation can drive people further away from God. Relationship should both precede and follow confrontation.

The cell church focuses on and gives opportunity for relational evangelism. It attempts to build relationships with unbelievers in a non-threatening environment. Unbelievers are exposed to Christ in the lives of believers and are exposed to the church through cell groups as they meet in the informal setting of believers' homes rather than a service at the church building.

Church life should be fun, rewarding, and enjoyable. The cell church gives you more freedom to exercise your God-given talents and spiritual gifts, so that you are spending more time doing the things that God created you to do and be, and less time conforming to the structures and traditions of men and churches.

The Cell Church Structure

The cell church is founded upon Jesus Christ with the cell groups as the focal point of the church. Church life is centered around the *cells* which meet in homes of members. The cell groups are organized into *congregations*. The role of the congregation varies from church to church. In some churches, the congregational organization is almost transparent. In these churches, the cells are organized into zones and districts which enables the church to manage the ministry and growth of the cells. In other churches, the cells are organized into satellite congregations that worship, equip, and minister together on a weekly basis.

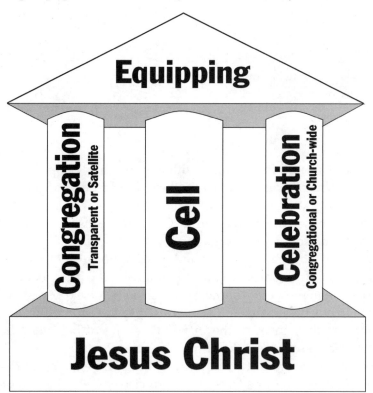

The congregations come together regularly for a *celebration* to God. Churches with transparent congregations come together for a church-wide celebration each week. In churches with satellite congregations, each congregation will have its own time of celebration. Then, about once a quarter, all the congregations come together for a joint celebration of God.

The *equipping* ministry of the church covers all aspects of church life. It disciples church members and provides the organizational structure which the church needs to accomplish its purpose. Thus the cell church has a single foundation with a four part structure: cell, congregation, celebration, and equipping (as illustrated).

Cells are the organism of the body of believers in small groups for the purpose of worship, experiencing God, ministering to one another and ministering to and evangelizing the community.

The cell church is built around the cells that meet in the homes of members. As you will learn in this book, the cell groups are vastly different from Sunday School classes.

This four tier structure creates an illusion that the cells, congregation, celebration, and equipping are equal partners in cell church structure and life. They are not. The cell is the basic unit of cell church life; the cells are the church. Rather than being an additional program or support to the congregational meeting, the cells are the basic unit of church life. They are distributed throughout the community in which they live in order to accomplish their ministry of rescue. The church is people in relationship (to one another and to God), not buildings, not programs, not meetings. In a cell church, everything else revolves around and is organized around the cells.

The purpose of a cell group is *to create a Christian fellowship with one another and God that lives among the non-Christian community; to let the Light of Christ shine through each member in order to touch the lives of those around them; to bring them to the feet of Jesus and the fellowship of His body, the church; and to teach them to walk in His steps.*

Congregations are the organization of cells into localized or homogeneous groupings in order to manage the ministry and growth of the cells.

Cell members in churches with transparent congregations will have a limited awareness of the congregational structure. The cells are organized into congregations in order to manage the ministry and growth of the cells. There may be few if any meetings of the congregation.

On the other hand, cell churches with satellite congregations may worship in different locations. In many urban areas, large worship spaces are very expensive. Satellite congregations provide worship services closer to where church members live at much less cost to the church. Other satellite congregations may organize according to different language groups, ethnic groups, or worship styles that meet the needs of a particular group of people.

Each satellite congregation will have its own worship and training time each week. When a satellite congregation outgrows its worship space (which ranges from 50-200 depending upon the size of the available facilities), the congregation will multiply into two congregations. This ensures an informal relational quality to the worship services that includes various types of participation and sharing during each of the different services. Congregations may be composed of people who speak different languages, of people located in a particular neighborhood, or people with other things in common (homogeneous). There is no limit to the number of congregations a cell church may have.

Some cell churches have a mixture of congregational forms. The most common mixture is a church with a large central congregation that has a transparent congregational structure. In addition to the primary congregation, there may be many satellite congregations as well.

Does your church have transparent congregations or satellite congregations? Check the appropriate response.

_____ Transparent Congregations
_____ Satellite Congregations
_____ Both
_____ Not sure

———— ❖ ————

Celebration is the gathering together of the church to experience and worship God.

———— ❖ ————

The traditional church usually has worship at 11:00 a.m. on Sundays in their sanctuary. The service is usually somewhat evangelistic in nature. The entire church usually comes together for this weekly service in a large sanctuary built for this one purpose. Often there is a second service on Sunday evenings that is focused more toward encouragement and instruction of the most faithful members.

In the cell church, celebration is one dynamic service that meets for about 90 minutes for worshipping God and encouraging and building up the church members. The time and day are less important. The church usually meets when ever and where ever it can locate a space large enough for the people to meet. In churches with transparent congregations, celebration space must be provided in one facility. Usually there are multiple worship services to maximize the use of the facilities. Churches with satellite congregations will have a celebration time for each congregation.

The celebration time in a cell church is for believers, not unbelievers. Unbelievers who attend will experience the presence and power of God, but they won't always be comfortable with what they experience. This service differs from the popular approach found in the "seeker" service where churches attempt to ensure unbelievers will not be confronted by anything uncomfortable. While this approach has its own strengths and weaknesses, it is different from the pure cell church where evangelism is primarily done through the cells, not during the celebration time.

The celebration time should be participatory in worship, praise, intercessory prayer, encouragement, and instruction. There is no need for a evening worship service that drains people of their time for ministry and fellowship with unbelievers.

Churches with satellite congregations should occasionally come together to celebrate what God has done and to worship Him together as one body. This is most often done on a quarterly basis.

Does your church have weekly celebration as a congregation or church-wide? Check the appropriate response.

_____ Congregational Celebration
_____ Church-wide celebration
_____ Both
_____ Not sure

Celebration, congregation and cell refer to the small, medium, and large structures of the cell church. As you can see, the cell church is decentralized in order to reach out into the community where people live. The first way in which it is decentralized is on the congregational level. The congregations are located according to where people live, or according to language, ethnicity, worship style, or other common denominators that will enable the congregation to reach a specific group of people.

The church is decentralized even further through the small cell groups that are located in homes, the work place, or where ever people can gather together.

As illustrated on page 22, the foundation of the cell church is Jesus Christ. On this foundation is the church structure of celebration, congregation and cell. The cell group is the center of church life. As the cell groups begin to multiply, they are organized into congregations. In a new cell church, the congregation and celebration are basically the same thing.

As the church continues to multiply cells, it may also multiply its congregations. As illustrated on the following page, the church has multiplied into three congregations. From the Original Congregation, it has multiplied into another congregation called Lake Side Congregation, and has started a Mandarin Speaking Congregation that meets at the same place the Original Congregation meets. After the church has multiplied into more than one congregation, there will also be times in which all the congregations will meet together for a church-wide celebration.

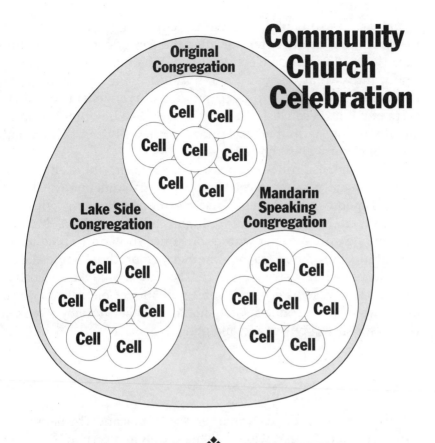

❖

Equipping refers to the administration of the knowledge, relational, servanthood and ministry skills, as well as the physical and spiritual resources needed for the church to accomplish its purpose.

❖

In addition to cell, congregation and celebration, the church must also have an equipping ministry to be a healthy church. You might refer to the equipping ministry as a covering or umbrella over the church's pillars. Before the church structure can accomplish its purpose, the people must be equipped and resources must be provided.

This includes such things as discipleship, training, Bible study, prayer, fellowship, ministry, and church administration.

Usually in a cell church, there is an equipping time for church members that meets before or after the congregational worship time. It would include elective classes for members, depending upon individual needs. There would be classes for new members, Bible study, prayer, missions, evangelism, discipleship, etc. But these classes would not need to be organized into small groups, with the exception of the children. The small group structure is in the cells.

There is also one-on-one discipleship in the cell group church. Usually, when a cell member leads someone to Christ, the cell member continues a discipleship relationship with the new convert. Much of the equipping in cell church life is through one-on-one apprenticing where someone who knows how to do something shows and teaches another person those same skills.

The prayer ministry of the cell church should be extensive. Prayer breakfasts for men and women, monthly Concerts of Prayer, and days of prayer and fasting should be called to empower the church for special power and anointing.

More Than Just a Name

The name of your cell groups is very important. The name will have connotations that will drive the group in a certain direction. If you call your cells *Care Groups*, the groups will tend to have an inward focus on fellowship and caring for group members. While this is good, it does not accomplish one of the ultimate objectives of the cell, which is drawing unbelievers to Christ. Another common name is *Home Bible Study Fellowships*. This makes the focus of the group the study of the Bible, which is little more than a Sunday School class meeting in a home.

Better names that may focus people away from looking at themselves might be *prayer cells*, *ministry cells*, or *shepherd groups*. In order to emphasize the evangelistic thrust of the cells, they might be called *evangelism cells*, but a cell is more than evangelism. In order to prevent having a name that denotes an inward focus, many people just call them *cells*. This may be the safest choice of names.

Potential Weaknesses of the Cell Church

Just as there are potential weaknesses to the traditional church structure, there are also potential weaknesses that may create problems in the cell church. A knowledge of these problems can help us guard against them.

1. The first area is doctrinal integrity. Because of the decentralization of the cell church, there is always the potential for some cell groups to venture off into doctrinal extremes. The apostle Paul struggled with this in his ministry which was composed of cell churches. This must be guarded against through maintaining direction and authority over cell group leaders, particularly through the supervision of Zone Servants and Zone Pastors (the organization of the cell church will be discussed in detail in later chapters). The church must react quickly and decisively to stop the spread of cancerous cells.

2. Another potential problem is emotionalism. Meeting in small groups in homes, depending upon the ministry of the Holy Spirit, discussing real problems of life, and worshipping God in an informal setting create a mix that will elicit more feeling and emotion than is usually experienced in traditional church life. This is a natural and good thing, but we must maintain a balance and not go to extremes. Orderliness and reasonable control must be maintained in cell group life.

3. Dependence upon experience rather than the foundation and authority of the Word is a potential problem in cell church life. The traditional church has become so focused on a cognitive knowledge of the content of the Bible, it has trapped many traditional churches into becoming hearers and not doers of the Word. While the cell church focuses on the doing of the Word, there is the opposite trap of focusing on the doing without maintaining a relationship with God through His Word. Although the cell group should not become a Bible study, it must hear from God through His Word. There must also be accountability and encouragement for church members to be involved in the daily

reading of the Word as individuals and families. There will also be large group equipping times that will focus upon the study of the Word. Finally, the celebration or congregational worship times in the cell church should rely upon expository (verse by verse) messages that are built upon the Word of God. This is important to maintain a proper balance of both hearing and doing the Word of God.

4. Because the cell church has a decentralized structure, there is always the potential for loss of control and accountability with a cell servant who strays from the mission and practice of the church. When this happens, the offending cell servant must submit to the authority of the body. If they do not, they must be removed. As David Yonggi Cho suggests, if there is a cancer in the body, surgical removal restores the body to health.

5. One final concern is stagnation. Any cell group that does not make the transition from self-centeredness to others-centeredness, or loses their vision and passion for reaching people for Christ will stagnate and begin to seek its own end. Such groups must be broken up and redistributed to healthy vibrant cells.

The CELL TEAM Shares

❖

What is the basic unit of the cell church? How does this differ from the traditional church?

What is the purpose of a cell group?

What are your cell groups called?

What function does this name imply or emphasize?

How will your cells guard against the weaknesses inherent in a cell group church?

What is your initial reaction to the cell church vision?

2

Basic Christian Community

❖

What is Community?

W hen you hear the word community, what thoughts come to mind? Does this word excite and motivate you or do you just shrug your shoulders in indifference? For many the word community brings to mind a quiet little village or neighborhood. If it does for you, then you need a completely new way of looking at community.

Think of a living organism in all of its intricate beauty and wonder. Millions of living cells are hard at work at very complicated and specific tasks. Neurons pass signals from the brain to orchestrate the symphony of life. Blood cells deliver oxygen and nutrients to each cell in exchange for the waste products of life. Specialized cells produce enzymes, convert amino acids, cleanse the blood, digest the food, transfer oxygen, fight intruders, and maintain delicate balances. All of this is community. Without the interdependence, co-operation, communication, and balance of these millions of living cells, the community of cells will die.

As community is necessary for life itself, community is necessary for living beings. A single individual may live their life in isolation, but if all the individuals of a species live in isolation, the species will become extinct.

Living in community is even more important for human beings. God created us to live in community with one another. Community takes place when three or more individuals agree to enter a joint relationship of interdependence. Those who are a part of a community agree to cooperate with one another in a way that is mutually beneficial to all parties.

People who become a part of a community also have certain common interests, ideals, and goals. Most neighborhood communities work together to provide things like food, protection, education, water, sewage, and recreation for the members of the community. In order to do this, each person must give up something to be a part of the community. They may have to pay taxes and give up certain individual rights to government authorities, but they are willing to do this because this arrangement benefits every member of the community.

According to the New Testament, the church is also based upon community. Each member of a local church community should agree to enter into a relationship with God and other believers that is mutually beneficial to all parties. The cell church represents the purest expression of relationships that God intended for His people to experience. The cell group is where you enter the community of God's family. To fully appreciate the significance of this family relationship, you must understand the communal nature of God, people, and the church.

God as Community

Scripture teaches us that God is one God, yet expresses Himself to us as the Father, the Son, and the Holy Spirit. Why has the one true God chosen to express Himself to us in three different ways? At least one of the reasons is that the triune God is an expression of community. Community is part of the perfection of God and all that He created. Part of the nature of God is community.

The Father, Son, and Holy Spirit work together in different yet interdependent ways. God the Father is the source of all things and has spiritual authority over all things. When man's sin caused a separation between God and man, the Father reached out to us by revealing Himself to us in the form of a man. While the Father sent His son into the world, the Son allowed His undeserved death to become a sacrifice for our sins. Together, they provided a way for man to come back into a personal relationship with God. We talk with the Father in the name of Jesus.

As humans, we can best understand and relate to God by looking at God's expression of Himself through Jesus. Jesus said, I and the Father are one (John 10:30). If you have seen me, you have seen the Father (John 14:9). Jesus has a perfect relationship with the Father and desires for us to be one in relationship with each another and with God.

> *. . . that they may all be one; even as Thou, Father, art in Me, and I in Thee, that they also may be in Us; that the world may believe that Thou didst send Me. (John 17:21)*

When Jesus left earth to sit at the right hand of God, Jesus depended upon the Holy Spirit to bring us into community with God. Jesus sent the Holy Spirit to live in our lives, i.e., God in us. The Holy Spirit provides a channel of communication between Jesus and ourselves. The Holy Spirit communicates the will, the power, and the fellowship of Christ to us. The Father, Son, and Spirit work through community.

Because of the community of the Trinity, we don't just know about God, we can commune with God. Because God lives in all Christians, communion with God also means communion with God's people. As we enter into community with God, we establish

interdependence. God's plan to bring His creation back into community with Himself is dependent upon His working through us. God has chosen to accomplish His redemption of mankind through His church.

Man and Community

Community is part of our human nature. From the point of birth, we live in an environment of community. The newborn child is totally dependent upon his or her parents for survival. As we grow up, we receive food, clothing, and shelter from our parents. We learn to speak, relate, live and love through the community of family. This is God's way for us. We are not independent creatures. There is no such thing as a normal fulfilled life apart from relationship with our earthly family and community.

As new believers in Christ Jesus, we are a new creation. We actually shed our old life and new life in the Holy Spirit begins. Our spiritual birth brings with it a need for spiritual community in a way similar to our need for earthly community.

We cannot live a normal fulfilled life apart from our relationship with God and our spiritual family.

The Church as Community

When we trust in Jesus, we are born into God's family. As we read the book of Acts, we are better able to understand the significance of what it means to be part of His family.

Prior to Pentecost, Jesus gathered the disciples together and told them to go to Jerusalem and wait for the coming of the Holy Spirit. During that time, they were of one mind in a community of fellowship and prayer. If we share common goals, submit to others for the common good, and spend quality time with one another, then community and oneness will result. After the disciples learned to be of one mind with each another, God joined their fellowship at Pentecost. God's participation and communion turned this band of disciples into a force that changed the world forever.

As we continue in the book of Acts, we discover that community is expressed through the cell groups of the first century church.

So then, those who had received his word were baptized; and there were added that day about three thousand souls. And they were continually devoting themselves to the apostles' teaching and to fellowship, to the breaking of bread and to prayer. And everyone kept feeling a sense of awe; and many wonders and signs were taking place through the apostles. And all those who had believed were together, and had all things in common; and they began selling their property and possessions, and were sharing them with all, as anyone might have need. And day by day continuing with one mind in the temple, and breaking bread from house to house, they were taking their meals together with gladness and sincerity of heart, praising God, and having favor with all the people. And the Lord was adding to their number day by day those who were being saved. (Acts 2:41-47)

In Acts 8:1, the Christians were thrown out of the temple and most of them were dispersed from Jerusalem. The early church growth that turned the known world upside down was an underground movement in the homes of believers. These first century Christians were eating meals and having fellowship from house to house. They were praying to God, praising God, ministering to people's needs, and learning about God. God's presence was demonstrated through the signs and wonders that were taking place. As they were filled with the Holy Spirit, they were speaking the Word of God with boldness, reaching others for Christ, and bringing them into the cell group fellowships of the church. All of this was done in cell groups that experienced the community of fellowship with God and with each another.

Basic Christian Community

The basic building block of society is the small group we describe as family. The basic building block of Christian community is the small group described in Acts. Today, these small groups have been rediscovered in the cell church.

The cell group is the perfect size to promote the interdependence of community. The intimacy of community breaks down when the size of a group exceeds 15 people. When Jesus chose His apostles, He chose 12 men to join Him in the interdependence of community. All of the elements of communion with God in the body of Christ are experienced at their best in the fellowship of the cell group.

Becoming part of a cell group is like being part of a new extended family. The cell group members become your spiritual family. Scripture is full of references to the family nature of our life in Christ. When our family went to the mission field in 1979, we left our parents, brothers, sisters, and other relatives. When we arrived in Malaysia and Singapore, we became members of what was referred to as the 'mission family.' Although we didn't understand it at the time, the other missionaries of our denomination in Malaysia and Singapore would become like family to us. Missionary children referred to my wife and me as Aunt Linda and Uncle David. Our children referred to the other missionaries as aunts and uncles as well. As we began to live, work, and minister together, our mission family took the place of our earthly family while we were there. Many years later we still consider many of those co-workers as family.

In our human families, infants learn how to live by watching and imitating their parents, brothers, sisters, relatives, and neighbors. It is the same in our spiritual families. As new babes are born into the family of God, they observe and learn from their spiritual fathers, mothers, sisters, and brothers. Paul says our relationship to other Christians should be like those in a good and wholesome family.

Do not sharply rebuke an older man, but rather appeal to him as a father, to the younger men as brothers, the older women as mothers, and the younger women as sisters, in all purity. (1 Timothy 5:1-2)

John also describes relationships within the body of Christ in family terms (1 John 2:12-14). As in an earthly family, there is an interdependence between each member of the cell family. Each person must do their part so the cell can accomplish its purpose. Every part is important. Accountability, responsibility, authority and submission are all a part of the community of family.

Each cell group is led by the cell servant and apprentice. Usually these are the spiritual fathers of the cell. They are not the bosses of the group, but they lead by serving and modeling. Within each cell, there are those who are mature spiritual fathers and mothers who provide wisdom and counsel to the young men and women in the cell. Whenever someone is brought into the group as a new believer, this newborn baby is discipled by the person who led them to Christ. The less mature grow in the faith by modeling their lives after (1) the Christ in Scripture, (2) the Christ in the lives of their spiritual parents, and (3) the Christ that lives in them.

One of the primary functions of the family is reproduction. Cell members involve themselves in building relationships with unbelievers in order to reach them for Christ. They draw them into the fellowship of the cell group that multiplies into two cell groups. Through evangelism and reproduction, the cell members work to complete what Christ began upon the Cross by bringing mankind back into a right relationship with the Father.

Family Tensions

While a healthy family is rooted in love, discipline, teaching, and cooperation, a normal family also has arguments, hardships, and disagreements. The cell family is not immune to these problems. A cell group is made up of imperfect people. The cell will begin as an immature group and it takes time, hardships, and conflict to mold the group into that which Christ desires it to be. There are many tensions the cell group will face during its lifetime.

One of these tensions is the different perceptions of what family life is about. Some people have never experienced a normal healthy family. Those from dysfunctional families don't want to have another family based upon their experience. They may not have had a father and mother who loved, cared, and provided for them. Those with fathers who were selfish, cruel, or abusive find it hard to identify with God as their Father. It will take these individuals time to learn what love in community is all about. The cell members must patiently and consistently love these wounded people and show them what it means to be a part of a loving family.

Another tension is the uncertainty of new relationships. When a new cell is formed, most individuals will approach these new relationships with apprehension. You really don't know these people. Questions arise like: "Can they really be trusted?

Will they like me, accept me, take advantage of me, or laugh at me?" As the new group begins to communicate with one another, conflicts will develop. Group members must learn to relate to different personalities. How do you know when a person is teasing or when they are serious? It takes time to learn about one another before the cell can really begin to trust one another. The members must listen and communicate with others and learn what they really mean, not just what we think they say. It also means that each group member may have to change something about themselves in order to bring harmony to the group.

Tensions are a normal part of the group process. Certain aspects of learning, growing, and adapting can only come about through conflict. Sometimes it may take open conflict or a crisis to bring the true feelings of those in conflict out into the open. Most of us live our lives with masks on, trying to hide our real identity. In the cell groups, we must learn to take our masks off and expose ourselves to God and each other. Conflict in the cell is resolved through the Holy Spirit, communication, love and trust. If we choose to love one another and make allowances for differences, the group will grow into communion and dependence upon one another.

Another tension in the life of a family occurs when the children grow up and leave the home to start their own families. If this event does not take place, the family lineage stops and the family dies. The life cycle of a cell group goes through this experience on a regular basis. Cell group multiplication creates tension, yet it is the essence of what happens in a healthy cell church.

There are also external tensions that a cell group will face. The primary enemy of the cell is Satan. When cell members begin to do the work of evangelism, Satan will attack the cell and its members in order to protect those in the kingdom of darkness from rescue into the kingdom of light. Cells whose members depend upon their own power and strength instead of the Holy Spirit may become casualties. Those who persevere will allow God to use the attacks of Satan for God's purpose. The trials will draw the family members closer to one another. Through mutual love and support, cell members will grow in their peace, joy and power. It will make them stronger and more determined to complete God's purpose for them.

Tensions are part of the sandpaper that God uses to shape and refine the cell group. They should not be considered as intruders. Unless we are willing to be changed, God cannot mold us into vessels that are fit for His purposes. As the group moves forward, the Holy Spirit will bond the group into a cohesive unit if the group will allow the Holy Spirit to control their lives.

Entering the Community

After a person has become a member of the cell group, how does one enter into the community of the cell? By way of review, here are six suggestions on how to enter into the community of the cell:

1. Before you can enter into the community of the cell, you must be in communion with God. Ways in which we commune with God include prayer, reading God's Word, and allowing the Holy Spirit to minister in and through our lives. This will be discussed in more detail in chapters three and four.

2. Entering into community always involves giving something up. Likewise in the cell, it means placing God as the number one priority in your life. It means placing your ambitions and goals behind your primary goal of serving Christ (Galatians 2:20). The primary channel of serving Christ is through the cell.

3. Commit yourself to make an investment of your time in the lives of the cell members. Spend quality time with cell members. Share meals with them, fellowship with them, and work together with them in the ministry of the cell group.

4. Choose to love everyone in the cell group from the beginning. Determine beforehand to make allowances for others and their differences. Patiently resolve conflicts and pray daily for each member.

5. Make yourself vulnerable to the group. Open your life up to the cell community so that you will be changed.

6. Commit yourself to the ministry of the cell. Be willing to do your part in serving others through ministry, relational evangelism, share groups, and other cell group ministries. Become a part of the team.

Conclusion

In review, the cell group is not a meeting; it is an experience founded upon relationships in which we become dependent upon one other. This includes our relationship with and dependence upon God. Through the Holy Spirit and the cell group, God takes our lives and works to remold us into the image of His Son. When problems arise in our lives, we are not alone. Because of the interdependence of our lives with God and our cell family, there is no obstacle too big to overcome. As cell members continue to grow in Christ, they join together on a mission with Christ to rescue men and women from the kingdom of darkness and bring them into the wonderful family of God.

The Cell Team Shares

———— ❖ ————

Ask team members to briefly share their own family backgrounds.

Discuss the positive aspects of a healthy family.

How is a cell group like a family?

Discuss the nature of community in the life of a cell group. In what way is God part of that community?

How do the tensions and problems of cell life contribute to community and unity?

Have you ever experienced this type of community? Briefly describe positive experiences of community in small groups.

Section Two

Spiritual
Foundations

3

Spirit-Filled Service

❖

Christin You

The cell group ministry is a channel for reaching large numbers of people for Jesus Christ. It is an effective tool as we head into the 21st century to fulfill the Great Commission throughout the world. One factor that makes the cell group ministry so effective is that it uses the principles of evangelism found in Scripture. A few of these principles are listed below.

1. We are to actively pursue those who are lost, to be fishers of men. (Matthew 4:19)

2. We must minister and care for the needs of people as Christ showed us through His ministry. (Matthew 10:42)

3. There is power in the New Testament Christian fellowship. (Acts 2:40-47)

4. We are all Priests, and must carry out the basic function of mankind's redemption together, i.e. we are all evangelists. (1 Peter 2:5,9)

5. The light of Christ must shine through us for the world to see. (Matthew 5:16)

As a leader or member of this dynamic evangelistic thrust, we cannot depend upon our own strength. If we allow *self* to rule on the thrown of our lives, we have no power other than our own. Occasionally we let *self* creep back upon the throne without being aware of it.

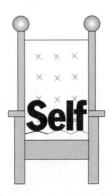

As Christians, we must daily choose between *self* on the throne . . . and CHRIST on the throne.

If we want to be a vessel of Him in cell groups, we must choose to allow Christ to rule on the throne in our lives. This means that we become a channel for Him to accomplish His purpose. In each of the following sentences, put the correct words in the proper blank.

It is not what I do _____ Christ that counts, but what

Christ does _____ me.

KEY WORDS: for, through

Spiritual productivity is not dependent upon _____ but

my _____ .

KEY WORDS: activity, availability

Have you made the choice clearly in your heart? Many of you already have. In preparation to minister in a cell group, let's reaffirm that decision in our lives (Galatians 2:20).

> **I claim that I have been crucified with Christ. It is no longer I who live, but Christ lives in me, and the life I now live in the flesh, I live by faith in the Son of God who loves me, and delivered Himself up for me.**
>
> ———————————————
> (Your Signature)

Obedience to Christ

If we have made the choice clearly in our lives that we will let Christ take complete control with no conditions attached, there follows an obedience to His will according to Scripture. As shown in the following diagram, obedience is part of a Christ-controlled Christian's life.

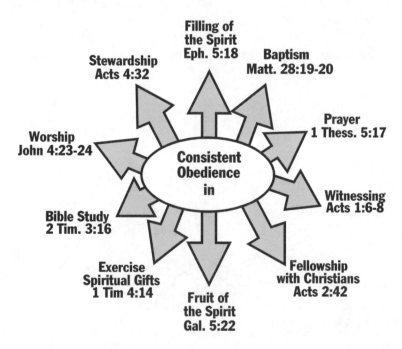

Now that you have made the decision to let Christ rule in your life, how does He do it? Through the Holy Spirit!

> *But I tell you the truth, it is to your advantage that I go away; for if I do not go away, the Helper shall not come to you; but if I go, I will send Him to you . . . But when He, the Spirit of truth, comes, He will guide you into all the truth; for He will not speak on His own initiative, but whatever He hears, He will speak; and He will disclose to you what is to come. He shall glorify Me; for He shall take of Mine, and shall disclose it to you. (John 16:7, 13-14)*

Christ sent the Holy Spirit to dwell in our hearts. The Holy Spirit, however, does not have His own agenda. The Holy Spirit receives direction from Christ, then reveals to us what Christ wants us to do. If Christ is on the throne in our lives, then the Holy Spirit becomes the channel through which Christ lives out His life through us. This is what we refer to as the Spirit-filled life.

The Spirit-Filled Life

When we accept Jesus Christ as Lord and Savior, we are baptized in the Holy Spirit as the Spirit regenerates us and seals us until the day of redemption. We thus experience spiritual birth with God as our Father, just as surely as we were physically born into this world.

This filling of the Spirit provides the power necessary for Christ to work mightily through us to accomplish His will in our lives. There are three things necessary for this filling.

First of all, we must make room for the Holy Spirit in our lives. The Holy Spirit can't find room in our heart if it is full of unconfessed sin. Through prayer, we confess our sin and are cleansed (1 John 1:9). This cleansing makes room for the Holy Spirit to fill us.

Second, we must ask the Holy Spirit to fill us (Ephesians 5:18). This simple prayer is as important to our spiritual lives as breathing is to our physical lives. Pray for the filling of the Holy Spirit before each cell group meeting. Each morning, as you begin your day, pray for the filling of the Holy Spirit in your life.

Third, we need to ask the Holy Spirit to bear His fruit in our lives on a daily basis. These are things that are not natural for us in the flesh, but come from God.

Pray at the beginning of each day that the Spirit would bear this fruit in your life.

———————— ❖ ————————

Lord Jesus, I ask you to bear the fruit of the Holy Spirit in my life today. Bear the fruit of love, joy, peace, patience, kindness, goodness, faithfulness, gentleness, and self-control.

———————— ❖ ————————

Spiritual Gifts

The gifts of the Holy Spirit are a very important part of what makes a cell group work. Through the exercising of spiritual gifts, the body of Christ accomplishes its mission of rescuing souls. Spiritual gifts are not something we take pride in as something we possess. It is that which God does through us.

The issue of spiritual gifts is one of the more controversial areas among evangelical Christians. The following section is not intended to be the final word regarding spiritual gifts in the cell church. The subject is too complicated to do a thorough biblical study in this book. It is intended to introduce the subject and provide an overview of some of the basic ways that spiritual gifts can be used in cell group life. The following gifts are taken from Romans 12:6-8, 1 Corinthians 12:28, and Ephesians 4:11. In discipleship training in your church, this area should be dealt with in more detail than is provided here.

Servant Gifts

The ministry of the cell group is empowered and led by the Holy Spirit. The cell servant serves the group through spiritual gifts, not through personal leadership abilities. Some of the gifts tend to empower the leadership of the cell groups more than others. For our purposes, we will describe these as servant gifts. Cell group servants (leaders) will usually exhibit at least one of the servant gifts. Cell group members may also possess some of these gifts. This is not to say that a single gift or category of gifts should be used as a litmus test for a cell group servant.

The Gift of Leadership is the ability to lead and shepherd a group of believers. This leadership is based on servanthood as will be discussed in a later chapter.

The Gift of Encouragement is an ability to encourage and challenge others, to comfort in times of distress, and to motivate people to do the will of God.

The Gift of Administration enables one to organize and delegate the ministry of the cell group.

The Gift of Teaching enables a member to teach, disciple, and/or apprentice others. This includes modeling and walking along with someone, not just lecturing.

The Gift of Prophecy; "Thus saith the Lord!" This gift is interpreted in a variety of ways according to various church traditions. It may be debatable as to its role in cell group life. One possibility from a cell group perspective would be that it may be a gift of vision that is sourced in God and verified by group concensus and the Word. Another might see this gift as a gift of proclaiming and expounding upon Scripture. Some would not see it as a servant gift at all.

"Body" Gifts

Certain gifts tend to empower group members in their ministry to one another and to those in the world. They are exercised in the context of the cell group and its work.

The Gift of Serving refers to the giving up of one's life in the service of others. The word literally means 'table waiting,' which implies even the most basic tasks in serving other people. Some people refer to this as the gift of hospitality. While it may include hospitality, it can often mean something more than what the term hospitality usually implies.

The Gift of Helping Others in Distress is a God sourced empathy toward those in misery which results in action.

The Gift of Faith is a rock or foundation within the group that is unshakable. When life's situations are difficult or seem hopeless, those with this gift strengthen the whole group. They have confidence that God is in control.

The Gift of Wisdom offers ministry and counsel to the body. This gift refers to wisdom in recognizing problems and giving wise counsel. This gift can also be used as a leadership gift in making wise decisions for the church or cell group.

The Gift of Knowledge is a knowledge and understanding of the things of God, particularly an understanding of God's Word. This knowledge can discern something in this world or a person's life that, when shared, brings a person closer to God.

The Gift of Discerning Spirits is an awareness of that which is of God and that which is demonic. It provides protection to the group from any work of Satan against the group or those being ministered to by the group.

The Gift of Giving is an ability to impart one's God given possessions to meet the needs of others.

The Gifts of Healing brings God's healing hand into the body of Christ, in this case, the cell group. It may include physical, emotional, or spiritual healing.

The Gift of Miracles or works of power involve the movement of God's Spirit in response to the prayers of the saints. These miracles bring about circumstances for the sake of the gospel that are unexplainable or seemingly impossible.

Gift of Evangelism

There is no such thing as a gift of evangelism that some believers have and others don't. This has become a common excuse for Christians to think they don't have the "gift" of evangelism, and thus do not have the responsibility to tell others about Christ. The passage in Ephesians chapter 4 about the gift of the evangelist is from a list of office gifts or positions of leadership.

And He gave some as apostles, and some as prophets, and some as evangelists, and some as pastors and teachers, for the equipping of the saints for the work of service, to the building up of the body of Christ; (Ephesians 4:11-12)

There is the gift of the apostle, prophet, pastor and teacher, and the evangelist. These are offices of leadership in which the Holy Spirit gives a spiritual empowerment in order to accomplish the ministry of that office. The gift of the evangelist is a Spirit sourced gift to an individual in the church to equip Christians in the church for the work of evangelism. As an equipper, the person with the gift of evangelism will certainly be gifted in leading others to Christ. The role of this individual, however, is not to be the person in the body to do evangelism, but to demonstrate, motivate, and equip others in the body to do the work of evangelism. The Scriptures do not describe a spiritual gift of evangelism anywhere else. Granted, some people are more at ease and seem to be more effective in their witness than others. These people are empowered by the Holy Spirit in their witness. Although this empowerment may be expressed in different ways in people of different personalities, Holy Spirit empowerment for witnessing is something God offers to all believers.

Each spiritual gift is a Spirit sourced attribute that some believers have, while others do not. The New Testament admonishes every believer that we are all ambassadors for Christ. All are witnesses and should share our faith.

Gift of Tongues

While the Bible clearly teaches that the gifts are given for unity, ironically Satan has used the gift of tongues to cause division and disunity among believers. As far back as the church at Corinth, this gift has caused division in the body of Christ. That grieves God! Because of this controversy, many churches are afraid of using or emphasizing spiritual gifts, and thus are not fully equipped for ministry in the Body of Christ.

In response to the problems in the Corinthian church, Paul gave them guidelines for the use of tongues. Following Paul's example and for the sake of unity, your church should clearly provide biblical instruction in this area.

Your gifts

In the space below, write what you believe are your spiritual gifts. Be prepared to share these during a cell group meeting. If you don't know what your gifts are, ask close friends.

Priesthood of Believers

One of the more important concepts of the cell church is that every member ministers. No holy men exist (priests/pastors/clergy) who must serve as a buffer between our holy God and the poor ignorant sinful masses. Every believer has direct access to God, the Father, through Jesus Christ. As members of the church, all are part of a holy priesthood.

And coming to Him as to a living stone, rejected by men, but choice and precious in the sight of God, you also, as living stones, are being built up as a spiritual house for a holy priesthood, *to offer up spiritual sacrifices acceptable to God through Jesus Christ. (1 Peter 2:4-5)*

This passage indicates that all the members of the church are priests. What then is a priest? A priest is one who offers sacrifices to God. As members of the body of Christ, the sacrifice that God desires as our worship to Him is our lives (Romans 12:1-2). Thus we serve as priests to God by offering our lives to Him so that He may use us for His own purpose.

Many people use the principle of the priesthood of the believer to justify their desire for every Christian to believe whatever they want to believe. Our priesthood is built on a much stronger foundation. What does the Bible say about the purpose of this priesthood?

> *But you are a chosen race, a royal* priesthood, *a holy nation, a people for God's own possession, that you may proclaim the excellencies of Him who has called you out of darkness into His marvelous light; (1 Peter 2:9)*

As priests, we offer our lives to God as His own possession so that we may *proclaim the excellencies of Him who has called us out of darkness into His marvelous light*. Thus all the members of the body should collectively complete the mission that Christ began on the cross and will complete at the second coming. That mission is to rescue mankind from the kingdom of darkness and bring them into the glorious kingdom of God.

Many people see the church staff and pastors as hired professionals that are to do the work of the church. You will not find this in the Bible. The distinction between clergy and laymen is a church tradition that has some biblical basis, but its practice today is not based upon a clear biblical teaching. There are, however, spiritual gifts given to positions of leadership within the church. These positions are not for the purpose of serving as professional ministers or priests.

> *And He gave some as apostles, and some as prophets, and some as evangelists, and some as pastors and teachers, for the equipping of the saints for the work of service, to the building up of the body of Christ; until we all attain to the unity of the faith, and of the knowledge of the Son of God, to a mature man, to the measure of the stature which belongs to the fulness of Christ. (Ephesians 4:11-12)*

These leadership positions are Spirit empowered to *equip* the church members for the work of the ministry. The members are the priests and ministers! The truth that you are a priest and minister of the gospel of Jesus Christ is one of the foundational scriptural principles that makes the cell church the powerful evangelistic instrument that it is!

The Cell TEAM Shares

❖

What is the role of the Holy Spirit in the ministry of the cell group?

Ask each person in the cell group to identify their spiritual gifts, if they know what they are. Then for each person, ask other cell group members to identify that person's spiritual gifts as evidenced through their ministry and service.

Write down the spiritual gifts the group attributes to you in the space below. Pray daily that God will reveal, mature, and develop these gifts in your life.

What does the priesthood of the believer mean to you?

What guidelines has your church set up concerning the gift of tongues?

4

The Power of
Prayer

❖

The power behind the cell groups, your church, and your own life is the Holy Spirit. We access the power of the Holy Spirit through prayer. The church and cell group grounded in prayer will see dynamic works that only God can do. Without it, ministry will only become another activity of the flesh.

Before the Throne

When we pray to God, we come directly to the throne of the God of the universe in all His majesty, power, and glory. Yet we know that God is ready and waiting to commune with us through prayer. When we think about the awesome reality of such an encounter, it is marvelous to know that He waits upon us and desires to fellowship with us. The drawing on the next page illustrates this.

This illustration alone does not give us a balanced perspective of prayer. Prayer involves a paradox in that it is an awesome experience of coming before our glorious and majestic God. Yet in spite of its awesomeness, prayer brings us into an intimate and close fellowship with our mighty creator. It is often hard for us to imagine that such a powerful and mighty God can be so approachable and desires to fellowship with each of His children as He walked and talked with Adam and Eve in the garden. In spite of the greatness of God, through prayer we are brought into the inner circle to fellowship.

Some people are too fearful of such a mighty God to be comfortable in approaching Him in an intimate way. We are not to be fearful of God in the sense of terror. Our fear of God should entail respect, reverence, and awe. Many people cautiously approach God, not wanting to bother Him, then dial in the special code (Dear Heavenly Father), close their eyes, and deliver their petitions as if they were communicating over a one-way telephone line.

Another misconception of prayer is to view prayer as a duty. Prayer that is perceived as a duty is a burden. Powerful prayer is not sourced in our duty. It is a glorious, wonderful, and joyful relationship. With a lifestyle of prayer, we can commune with God with our eyes open, while driving the car, while eating a meal, while working, before making any decision, before meeting a new person, or any other time so we can know God's will for our lives in all things.

To truly understand what prayer is, we must balance the illustration on the previous page with the one demonstrated below. Study the following illustration representing the relationship between the believer and his Lord. How would you describe your own prayer life in light of these illustrations and this discussion?

When we begin to grasp prayer as a relationship, we begin to grow in our relationship with God and His Son, Jesus.

The power of your cell group will never rise above the power of the individual prayer lives of group members. You must grow and build a powerful prayer life in order to see God begin to work and empower your life for service and ministry from a personal to a global level. Begin asking Jesus now to teach you and motivate you to pray. What a wonderful and joyous experience it is to begin to fellowship with your creator in a more intimate and personal way.

Each time your cell group meets, you will not only fellowship with one another, you will also fellowship with God through praise and prayer. Group members will share their personal joys, hurts, and petitions in order to give the group an opportunity to share those joys, meet your needs as they can, and offer prayers of petition so that God's perfect will can be accomplished in your life. You will also pray for the ministries of group members and the church. Prayers for the salvation of specific individuals will be offered to God as the group is empowered to rescue souls from the kingdom of darkness into the kingdom of light.

From personal prayer to prayers in your cell group, your church will receive power. But you will also pray during the weekly celebration services of your church. Regularly, your church will gather together for corporate times of extended prayer where the entire time will be spent in prayer. You will begin to learn that personal intimacy with God through prayer will become a lifestyle of joy and relationship, rather than a burden laden with guilt.

As the church reaches out into the community through the cell groups and various ministries, they must support every effort through prayer. One of the best ways to engage in spiritual battle through prayer is to take the battle to the community. Prayer walks work well in doing this. Cell group members should periodically walk through their community while praying. Walking and jogging is commonplace worldwide and can be done without bringing attention to oneself. In groups of two or three, walk or drive through your community while praying, which can be done with your eyes wide open. Ask the Holy Spirit to expose the work of Satan to you, and then pray for specific people to be freed from Satan's bondage. For instance, you can look at someone's home and usually tell if they have a problem with materialism. Pray that the people in that home be released from the bondage of materialism.

Pray for the salvation of each person in that home using the guidelines in the conclusion of this chapter.

Note: See Appendix A for specific instructions for conducting prayer walks.

Prayer and Evangelism

The following is a careful study of Paul's teaching on evangelism. In this single paragraph of scripture (Colossians 4:2-6), Paul has given us powerful instruction on how to win people to Christ. The strategies implied in this passage are uniquely suited to evangelization through cell groups. First, read the whole passage.

Devote yourselves to prayer, keeping alert in it with an attitude of thanksgiving; praying at the same time for us as well, that God may open up to us a door for the word, so that we may speak forth the mystery of Christ, for which I have also been imprisoned; in order that I may make it clear in the way I ought to speak. Conduct yourselves with wisdom toward outsiders, making the most of the opportunity. Let your speech always be with grace, seasoned, as it were, with salt, so that you may know how you should respond to each person. (Colossians 4:2-6)

Now let's carefully break down these verses to see what Paul means.

First of all, in the context of evangelism, Paul says *"Devote yourselves to prayer."* The word for *"devote"* means to persevere continually. Prayer and evangelism go hand in hand. If we take evangelism seriously, we devote ourselves continually to prayer for the salvation of the souls God has brought into our paths.

We are also to *"keep alert in it."* *"It"* refers to our prayers. As we live out our life and in our daily walk, we should look for opportunities to let the light and joy of Christ shine through us. If you are alert in your prayer, before you talk to any stranger, or non-Christian acquaintance, utter a prayer for that person. In only a brief moment in your heart, you can pray that God would cleanse you of any sin that would be a hindrance to the work of the Holy Spirit, and pray that the Spirit would show you what to say and do so that this person might ultimately come to know Christ.

We are to pray *"with an attitude of thanksgiving."* What does it mean that our evangelistic prayers should be with an attitude of thanksgiving? As we pray evangelistically, we should pray with an attitude of expectancy for what God is going to do. We should be expecting results from our witness, praying with faith that our witness will not return to us empty and without effect. We should pray believing that God will work. If we do believe, then our faith will be accompanied by a prayerful attitude of thanksgiving to God for what He is doing, and is going to do.

"Praying at the same time for us as well." Here Paul is instructing us to pray for one another's witness. As we pray for our own evangelistic efforts, we should also pray for the witness of others in our cell groups. In the cell group, all of the members are praying specifically for the witness of each member and the salvation of specific individuals.

We've been talking a lot about prayer so far, but exactly what are we praying for? For one thing, we are praying *"that God may open up to us a door for the word."* God is the one who will provide the opportunity for us to witness to others. But we need to pray for those opportunities. Satan will do everything he can do to prevent these doors for the word to be opened for us. So we must do battle and pray for these opportunities. If we will pray, God will answer this prayer.

"So that we may speak forth the mystery of Christ." When the door has been opened, we must pray that the mystery of Christ will be revealed through our lives and words. It is not the words that you say that will reveal the mystery of Christ. Paul speaks of the message of Christ as a mystery because the truths of the gospel are foolishness to men. You cannot convince someone to become a Christian through your eloquent words. It is a mystery that can only be revealed through the Holy Spirit. The Holy Spirit works in our lives to show us what to say, but the Holy Spirit is also at work in the life of the unbeliever to translate what is said, convict them of their sin, reveal the truths of this mystery to them, and draw them to Christ.

"For which I have also been imprisoned." Paul warns us that our witness will be opposed. There is a real battle going on over our offensive attacks upon Satan's kingdom.

There is a parallel passage to Colossians 4:2-6 in Ephesians 6:18-20. Read both passages and note the striking resemblance.

How many words or phrases can you find that are similar?

Now read Ephesians 6:10-17. What is the context of this passage? Write your answer in the space provided.

Evangelism, spiritual warfare, and prayer are so intertwined that it is hard to separate them. Now let's return to our study of Colossians 4:2-6.

We should also be praying that the Holy Spirit will be in complete control of our witness so that everything we say will be exactly what that person needs to hear. So I should pray *"in order that I may make it clear in the way I ought to speak."* There is no one line or phrase that we should always use in our witness. Many times, we will say nothing directly about Christ. What do we say? How do we act? Only the Holy Spirit knows what that person needs to hear so we must trust Him to work through us.

"Conduct yourselves with wisdom toward outsiders." The word for *"conduct"* means *"to walk."* This is referring to our everyday walk of life. *"Outsiders"* refers to non-Christians. The core of our witness for Christ is carried on in our everyday walk of life. The people we meet at work, in our neighborhood, in our leisure activities, as we shop, and wherever we go should be the basis of our witness for Christ. As we meet these people, we should pray for wisdom that God will use us to draw them to Christ.

"Making the most of the opportunity" literally means *"redeeming the time."* As we meet people in our everyday walk, Paul is telling us that we should not let these opportunities be wasted. We should redeem these everyday interactions with non-Christians for the sake of the gospel. This is the heart of our witness. Most of us waste the time we spend in normal interactions with people we

meet each day. Don't let that time be wasted. Redeem that time for the gospel. The word *"time"* refers to a seasonal time. There is a right time and a wrong time. There is a right time to directly proclaim Christ, and there is a time when doing so would cause more harm than good. How direct or indirect should our witness be? As we go back to previous verses, we remember that the Holy Spirit knows the right thing to say and do so our witness will be effective.

"Let your speech always be with grace." As we meet non-Christians in our everyday walk, our speech should be gracious. The things we say, our body language, and our facial expressions communicate our true feelings toward the people we meet. When we pass people in our everyday walk, particularly in the cities, we are in a hurry. We really don't care about the people we meet. As far as we are concerned, they can literally go to hell. If we have an attitude of love, joy, and concern in our lives toward those we meet, we will certainly be noticed. When we demonstrate joy and concern, hurting people will be drawn to us.

"Seasoned, as it were, with salt." Our interaction with these unbelievers and our conversations with them should be seasoned with salt. There were many different uses of the word *"salt"* in New Testament times. The one that seems to fit here is the first century practice of using small amounts of salt as fertilizer. In our day of modern agriculture, it is hard for us to imagine any amount of salt being used as fertilizer, but it's true. In the context of this passage, we are sowing the seed of the gospel. Just the right amount of salt served as fertilizer for crops, but too much salt caused the ground to become infertile and grow nothing. It is the same way with our witness. How direct should our witness be? Should we present the plan of salvation to this stranger? Or should we speak kindly, smile, and just show our concern for them? Our presentation of God's love is just like using salt for fertilizer. If we use too much, that person will be offended, and the soil of their lives will be infertile to our witness. How do we know how much to use? The Holy Spirit will show us if we will ask Him.

"So that you may know how you should respond to each person." This last phrase is very important. It tells us two things. First of all, we should be responding, talking, and interacting with the people

we meet in our daily walk. But it also tells us that each person is unique. They have different needs, hurts, and understandings of Christianity. There is no one approach in our witness that we should use with every person. We must be sensitive to the Spirit's leading so that our witness will pierce the very heart of each unique unbeliever we meet.

In 1987, I was shopping for groceries in the state of Washington. While I was standing in the checkout line, I noticed that the checkout clerk looked extremely tired and distressed. The man at the counter was watching her very closely as if he were convinced that she was going to try and cheat and overcharge him. The man was abrupt and rude. I began to pray for that woman. What could I do or say that could be used of God as a witness to her? I prayed that the Holy Spirit would show me what to do. When my turn came, I told her that she must have one of the toughest jobs I could think of. She looked offended and said, "What do you mean by that?" I told her I had noticed how the man had given her a difficult time and she agreed. I said, "With all those long hours of standing, with everyone in a hurry and pressing you to go faster, and with people thinking you are trying to cheat them, this must be a very difficult job." She paused, and then agreed. She said her work was very hard and that she was very tired. Then she added, "You're the first person that's ever told me they appreciate what I do and understand how hard this job is." She smiled and said, "That really means a lot. Thanks."

The next time I went shopping, I looked to find that same lady. She was there, and I got in her checkout line. She looked tired and distressed as before. When she noticed me out of the corner of her eye, a smile came across her face. I don't remember what I said to her, but I gave her a word of encouragement and told her that I had been praying for her. I never saw that woman again, but I believe that some seed was sown that God has used.

I use this illustration as an example of the principles described in this verse. The time we spend to check out our groceries is a good example of wasted time that needs to be redeemed for the gospel.

As you study this passage, note the dependence of our witness upon prayer, the Holy Spirit, and our availability. Now reread this passage with new understanding.

*Devote yourselves to prayer, keeping alert in it with an attitude
of thanksgiving; praying at the same time for us as well, that God
may open up to us a door for the word, so that we may speak forth
the mystery of Christ, for which I have also been imprisoned; in
order that I may make it clear in the way I ought to speak.
Conduct yourselves with wisdom toward outsiders, making the
most of the opportunity. Let your speech always be with grace,
seasoned, as it were, with salt, so that you may know how you
should respond to each person. (Colossians 4:2-6)*

It is thrilling to practice the principles Paul gives us in this
passage. How do you measure up to Paul's instruction?

Personal Evaluation

Answer the following questions based upon what you have
learned in this chapter.

1. When you meet people during the day, are you praying and
   thinking about their salvation?

2. When people meet you, do they see the love and joy of Christ in
   your life? Explain.

3. Think of the last person you met who may not have been a
   Christian. Based upon the material on prayer and evangelism,
   evaluate your interaction with that person.

4. What are some concrete ways you can implement what you have just learned in this chapter as a part of your daily life?

5. Try to practice what you have learned for one full day. At the end of that day, write a diary of what happened. Was anything different in your life? Was anything different in the way people responded to you?

Prayers for Salvation

As a cell group, you must battle in the heavenlies for the salvation of souls before a harvest will be reaped. When you are praying for someone's salvation, include the following areas in your prayers.

1. Present the person by name to Jesus Christ as His purchased possession.

2. Pray against the powers of darkness that claim a hold on this person's life so that this person will have the freedom to choose to accept or reject Jesus Christ apart from Satan's interference or bondage.

3. Pray that the Holy Spirit will draw this person toward Christ, convict them of their sin, and reveal to them the truth of God's plan for salvation.

4. Pray God will bring circumstances, people, and events into this person's life in order to reveal to them their need for Christ.

5. Pray God will use you as an instrument to bring this person to Christ. Pray the Holy Spirit will guide your every word and deed so that you will say and do the right thing at the right time. Pray that the light and joy of Christ will shine through your life as a testimony of the Christian faith.

The Cell TEAM Shares

—————— ❖ ——————

Review the material on Colossians 4:2-6.

Ask team members to share what they learned about themselves in the personal evaluation.

Review the list on how to pray for the lost. Stress the importance of keeping unbelievers on our daily prayer lists.

Plan a prayer walk to be done during the following week. Discuss how you would conduct such a walk. What would you pray about?

Spend the remaining time in prayer. Pray for the salvation of specific unbelievers and for opportunities to share Christ with them as appropriate.

Section Three

Cell Group
Dynamics

5

Oikos Relationships

❖

Networks of Relationships

According to Tom Wolf of Church on Brady in Los Angeles, California, human groupings can be divided three ways: common kinship, common community, and common interest. In the New Testament, the word for these groupings is *oikos* or *household*. It comes from the word *oikonomos* which means a steward. Wolf defines an *oikos* as a social system composed of those related to each other through common ties and tasks. That includes such people as relatives, neighbors, co-workers, fellow students, friends, and those in special interest groups.

An *oikos* refers to relationships established through people with common interests, goals, problems, age, etc. The most natural way to win people to Christ is through one's *oikos*. In targeting groups of people for evangelism, particularly in an urban setting, you should discover the group's *oikos* systems, and develop strategies to penetrate them.

75

Actually there are five different types of relationships that describe people in your *oikos*: neighbors, relatives, common interests, common needs, and common tasks.

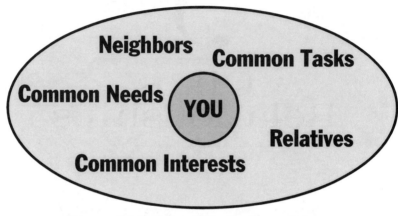

Your World of Relationships

Now that you know the types of relationships that determine your *oikos*, these relationships can be further clarified by looking at your personal oikos, your extended *oikos*, and your potential *oikos*.

Personal *Oikos* (8-10 people)

The most obvious and important *oikos* in your life is your personal *oikos*. An easy way to determine who is in your *oikos* and who is not is the average amount of time you spend with people in your daily life. We spend at least 30-45 minutes per week, on average, with the people in our *oikos*.

These are the people we relate to in our daily life. We usually have the trust and respect of these people. We can talk to them about things that we would probably not talk about with others. These are the people who are most likely to respond to our witness of Jesus Christ.

In the space provided, list the people in your personal *oikos* (Those you spend an average of 30-45 minutes or more per week in personal conversation or activity).

The average number of people in one's *oikos* is 8-10. This number varies depending on whether one is extroverted or introverted. Other factors are involved such as family size, work environment, length of residence, emotional state, etc.

In many churches, however, members only allow other Christians into their inner circle of *oikos* relationships. How many

Personal Oikos

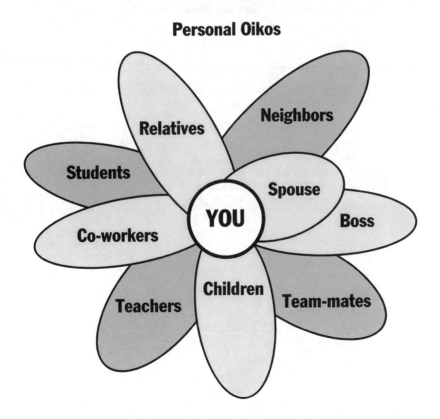

people on your list are probably not Christians? If we are to be a witness for Christ, we must work to bring non-Christians into our personal *oikos* in order to reach them for Christ.

Extended *Oikos* (50-200+ people)

Another way to view your *oikos* (in order to reach others for Christ) is your extended *oikos*. Your extended *oikos* refers to the *oikoses* of those who are in your *oikos* (see illustration below). Every person in your personal *oikos* has their own personal *oikos*. Some of these people may be the same as those in your personal *oikos*, but many will be different. There may be as many as 200 people in your extended *oikos*.

As you reach people for Christ in your own *oikos*, search through the *oikoses* of the people you reach in order to discover

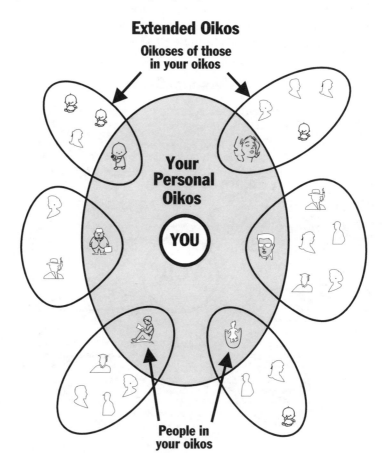

Extended Oikos

Oikoses of those
in your oikos

Your
Personal
Oikos

YOU

People in
your oikos

others who can be targeted for the gospel. The newly converted individual probably has non-Christian friends. This is a fertile field. When you reach people through your extended *oikos*, you also disciple the person in your own *oikos* to share the gospel.

Potential *Oikos* (Unlimited Number)

A final way to view our *oikos* relationships is by looking at potential *oikoses*. This refers to people you have not yet met who have the potential to become a part of your *oikos*. These are people with whom you have a *right to relationship*. A *right to relationship* is a culturally defined right to interact and communicate with another person who has a culturally defined obligation or desire to respond.

People in your potential *oikos* are people with whom you have a common interest or bond, that when discovered, creates a desire

Potential Oikos

Groups of People

to establish a conversation or limited relationship. For example, I am an avid basketball fan. My favorite college basketball team is the University of Kentucky. When I am wearing a shirt with the Kentucky insignia on it, Kentucky fans will identify themselves to me, and we will stop to talk about our mutual interest. This is true whether I am walking in a shopping mall or on a street in South Carolina, Washington, or Dallas, Texas. Whether I am in the Philippines or Jackson, Mississippi, if I go to a basketball court, many of the other players are a part of my potential *oikos*. If I am a good player, that likelihood is increased in proportion to my skills.

Sometimes being a neighbor gives me a right to enter someone's home to visit; in some places it does not. Usually living near someone means they are much more likely to visit with me than if I am a complete stranger from another neighborhood or town. But in some parts of the world, like Singapore, there are exceptions. Each part of the world has its own culturally defined rules as to what gives you a *right to relationship*, and what does not. These rules are important to learn.

In Singapore, the national past-time is eating. Eating out is where you entertain and visit with other people, not in people's homes. If I visit a coffee shop in Singapore, and the shop is empty except for a single person in the corner, it is usually alright for me to go over and sit down with that person to talk and eat. That's what you do in a Singapore coffee shop.

In America, suppose I go to a McDonald's restaurant, and there is only one person eating in the corner of the restaurant. If I go over and sit down beside this person, he or she will probably object. I would be invading their privacy. If I violate the cultural rules and force myself on people, I create barriers to the gospel rather than building bridges.

Common interests can also create a bond between people. For example, if I meet another person who is strongly opposed to pornography, and we share that cause in an area where it is a real problem, then we are comrades. Shared causes bring people together in relationship. There are many things that create a right to relate, and there are many things that build barriers to relationships. As we look to share the gospel, we must first build trust through the natural *rights to relationship* and avoid building barriers by forcing a relationship when no *right to relationship* has been established.

This principle is very important. Let's review it again.

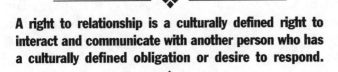

A right to relationship is a culturally defined right to interact and communicate with another person who has a culturally defined obligation or desire to respond.

Man of Peace

As you establish a *right to relationship* and enter into someone's household (*oikos*), look for the man of peace. The man of peace is described in Luke 10:

Now after this the Lord appointed seventy others, and sent them two and two ahead of Him to every city and place where He Himself was going to come. And He was saying to them, "The harvest is plentiful, but the laborers are few; therefore beseech the Lord of the harvest to send out laborers into His harvest. Go your ways; behold, I send you out as lambs in the midst of wolves. Carry no purse, no bag, no shoes; and greet no one on the way. And whatever house you enter, first say, 'Peace be to this house.' And if a man of peace is there, your peace will rest upon him; but if not, it will return to you. And stay in that house, eating and drinking what they give you; for the laborer is worthy of his wages. Do not keep moving from house to house." (Luke 10:1-7)

In this passage, Jesus is sending out His disciples to proclaim the coming of the kingdom. He is sending them into the cities and villages where they are to enter into households. The Greek word here is *oikos*. As they entered into an *oikos*, they were to look for a man of peace that God had already prepared to receive the disciples. These men of peace will be open to both the person and the message. When they found the man of peace, they were to stay in that *oikos* until their task was complete. If there was no man of peace, they were instructed to move on to another *oikos*.

If we will pray for open doors to our witness, the Holy Spirit will prepare the way for us. As we enter into an *oikos* other than our personal *oikos*, we should look for someone with whom we have a *right to relationship*. Pray the Holy Spirit will prepare them to receive us and eventually the message of the Gospel. This is the way we penetrate a new *oikos*. Once someone has been converted in that *oikos*, then that individual can reach their own *oikos* for Christ in a way that we cannot do alone. But we should stay in that *oikos* and continue to explore the complex web of *oikos* networks (relationships) to reach as many people as possible for Christ. If there is not a man (or woman) of peace in that *oikos*, we should move on to another.

The Cell TEAM Shares

—————— ❖ ——————

What is an *oikos*?

How many people are in all the personal *oikoses* of your cell group?

How many probable non-Christians are part of the personal *oikoses* of your cell group?

What are the implications (of the number of unbelievers in the *oikoses* of your cell group) for evangelism through your cell group?

What are some of the natural *rights to relationship* in your community that may allow or hinder your witness?

Allow each team member to share areas in their own life that would create *rights to relationship* that could be used for building relationships and sharing the gospel. List these as they are shared.

Are there any common *rights to relationship* among members of your cell group that several in your cell group could use together to build relationships with non-Christians?

How would you search for a man (or woman) of peace?

Discuss plans to use these *rights to relationship* to bring others into your personal *oikos*. How can these people be reached for Christ? What role will prayer play in reaching these people?

6

The Cell Group Meetings

❖

Where?

The cell church is designed to go where people are, instead of trying to get people to come to where the church is located. Thus the cell groups can meet anywhere you find people gathered together. This includes work places, schools, homes, restaurants, etc.

The best place is definitely in people's homes. The home provides a comfortable, non-threatening environment. Entire families can come to your home and get to know one another more intimately. Barriers are more easily broken down as your home expresses who you are through your belongings, tastes, photographs, and lifestyle. The group can move from house to house and really get to know one another. If the group doesn't meet in the homes during the evening, the problem of time may prevent the group from properly functioning. Not everyone can get a two hour lunch break from work, even if it is just one day a week. If the people you are trying to reach for the Lord can't meet at your planned time, you need to make a change.

If you meet in people's homes, you must decide whether to rotate homes or to regularly use a single home. Usually it is better to rotate homes as suggested above, but there are circumstances that may make this difficult. If some of the homes in your cell group are too small for the group to meet, it may be best not to rotate homes at all. Otherwise, the homes that are too small are singled out as deficient. If the cell group has numerous children, some homes may not have adequate space for both the children and adults. In this case, consider using one home for the adults and a nearby home for the children.

The children may also meet outdoors, in a basement, or in a garage. If there is only one home that has space for both children and adults, you may use that home regularly. An advantage of using a single home is that everyone always knows where the cell group will meet, but the disadvantages include the inconvenience to the family every week and the inability to get to know families better through interaction with those families in their natural habitat.

When?

The best time for the cell group to meet is whatever time is most convenient to those in the group. Since there is not a second worship service to attend in a cell church, many cell groups will choose Sunday evenings for cell group meetings. Some church strategies will be designed to get your people out into activities on Sunday either prior to or following your celebration time in order to build bridges with non-Christians. If this is the case, then don't meet in cell groups on Sundays. Any day of the week is fine, including Saturdays. If you meet in homes, an evening is preferable. If you meet at school or in the work place, choose the most convenient time for most of those in your group as well as your unreached target group. Students may meet after school or on weekends. In the work place, the lunch hour is the most likely choice. You may also meet before work begins and serve a light breakfast such as coffee and donuts.

Who?

The most common cell groups are composed of married couples. All male and all female groups are also an option that many churches are using. But there can also be cell groups designed to reach any ministry focus or target group. There can be cell groups composed of singles, single parents, college students, secondary students, workers, teen-agers, etc. Whatever group comprises the cell, each cell will attempt to reach people similar to themselves. Individual cell groups within the church might target different language or racial groups, people with similar needs or problems, or just people who live close to one another.

What?

A typical cell group meeting will last for about 90 minutes. The maximum time should be 2 hours. The group should begin and end promptly. The host of the meeting should plan for about 2 hours which includes arrival and fellowship time.

A cell group meeting is divided into six parts.

- *Ice Breaker*
- *Praise*
- *The Word*
- *Edification*
- *Evangelism*
- *Fellowship*

Let's look at each part individually.

Ice Breaker (10-15 minutes)
When you begin your cell group meeting, you need time to prepare group members to focus away from the worry and activities of the day and concentrate on the Lord and those in the group. This should be an activity that requires every person in the group to participate and open themselves up to the group. Some sample ice breakers may include such questions as:

What is the most important thing that happened to you during the last week? (This question can be used repeatedly, but others should be used occasionally as a change of pace.)

If you were to describe yourself as an animal, what animal would you choose and why?

What is your earliest remembrance in life?

Which of your material possessions has the most meaning to you and why?

With a 10 as outstanding, rate the quality of your day (or week) on a scale of 1 to 10. Briefly explain why you rated your day (or week) as you did.

The question should be simple and clear. Cell members should be able to answer in 1 to 2 minutes. The ice breaker portion of your meeting should last 10-15 minutes.

Praise (10-15 minutes)

Following the ice breaker, the next 10 minutes should be spent in praise and worship to God. The ice breaker brought team members away from the things of this world in order to focus on the members of the cell group. Now the focus needs to be on Christ and His presence through the work of the Holy Spirit.

Begin the praise time with a brief opening prayer. The opening prayer should be a prayer of praise. Ask for the presence of Christ (Matthew 18:20) and for the leadership of the Holy Spirit.

The major portion of the praise time will be spent in singing songs of praise to God. This does not include songs about God or the Christian life, but should be songs of praise directed to God. Usually hymns are about God. This may seem a minor point, but there is a big difference between singing about God and singing *to* God. Usually songs sung directly to God are short choruses or Scripture songs that we often associate with young people. Why is this so important? The praise time is actually a time of corporate worship where the group experiences the actual presence of a holy and living God. The corporate reading of scripture to God may also be used on occasion during this time. The leader of the praise time should carefully prepare the choice of songs and ensure that the 10-15 minutes does not turn into 20 or 30 minutes.

The Word (10 minutes)

This is a time of encouragement and instruction to the group. It may involve follow-up questions from the previous week's time of corporate worship. Coordination between the proclamation of God's Word during the weekly celebration time and the cell group meeting should be encouraged. It should include instruction or encouragement as read from Scripture. This time should not exceed 10 minutes. If it does, the group will revert to a Bible study and lose the dynamic of the whole concept of the cell group. This reading of the Word should be practical and helpful to group members in their daily lives.

The pastor of your church is responsible to provide weekly guidance to the cell servants for the content of this time.

There will be times when a cell group will need special training and instruction. This book might fall into this category. In such a case, the cell group will expand the overall time of the meeting up to 2 hours, and expand the Word period to 30 or 40 minutes rather than the usual 10. This, however, should not be a permanent extension of the length of the meeting.

The time in the Word should naturally lead into the edification time.

Edification (30-40 minutes)

The next 30 to 40 minutes will be a time of edification for the group. Edification refers to the process of spiritual enlightenment, growth, uplifting, or building up. It is a natural follow-up to hearing God's Word. Often, questions and discussions will be generated from the presentation of the Word or from the previous Sunday's message. There may be some pressing global or local crisis or issue that has captured everyone's attention. There may be a real crisis in the life of a cell member that the group will want to focus on as a beginning point. The cell servant should pray for wisdom and the leadership of the Holy Spirit in order to know how to initiate the time of edification. Whatever is discussed, the biblical perspective should be the focus. Whatever needs or personal problems come up, the group should minister to that person under the leadership of the Holy Spirit.

This is the core of the cell group meeting. This is a time of sharing and ministry by group members to one another and to visitors.

During the edification time, each cell group participant should have an opportunity to share their victories, trials, frustrations, and needs in order to receive counsel and prayer from the group. In newly formed cell groups, this time may begin awkwardly. You may need to go around in a circle to each person and ask them to share what is happening in their life. Ask them to focus on needs and prayer requests. Don't hesitate to stop and pray for each person after they have shared their needs. No cell member should leave the meeting with unresolved needs that have not been prayed over and discussed. Visitors should be encouraged, but not pressured, to share their needs for prayer as well.

As situations are discussed, if other group members have a word of wisdom or encouragement to give, they should give it in a caring and non-judgmental way. This is a time for the application of spiritual gifts to meet the needs of group members. Other gifts needed at this point might be a word of knowledge from the Scripture that gives guidance for the issue at hand, the gift of helping another in distress, or the gift of giving. If there is a physical, spiritual, or emotional problem for a group member, prayer should be offered for healing.

Cell members should be sensitive to the non-verbal communication of stress or anxiety by those in the group, including visitors. Those under stress should be encouraged, but not unduly pressured, to express their problems and receive insights from the group. Even if the problem is unspoken, there should be prayers offered for that person.

In a typical edification time, prayer items from the previous week would be shared by the Apprentice Servant who keeps a record of prayer needs. Answers to prayer may be noted and updates to previous prayer items given. This is often followed by prayer for the updated needs and praise for the answered prayers. Then new prayer concerns should be brought before the group. As each concern is expressed, give an opportunity for other members to empathize, give counsel or support as the Holy Spirit leads. Ask someone to lead in a prayer for that concern before moving on to others.

The group should regularly be reminded that by participating in the cell group each person is agreeing to keep the items shared confidential. When personal things are shared in confidence, they must be kept in confidence. Otherwise, people will not share their real needs before the group.

Evangelism (15-20 minutes)
This is a time of preparation, planning, and prayer for the work of the cell group. All team members should participate in this time. At least 15 to 20 minutes will be required to complete this function of the cell group.

Each cell group member should be developing their strategy for winning various people in their *oikos* to the Lord. Group members can assist one another in developing these strategies and pray for one another and for those who are being targeted for the gospel. Often, several members will find they have people in their *oikos* who would benefit from a joint ministry or event. The cell group can plan various evangelism projects as an individual cell or in conjunction with other cells. Much, but not all, prayer and planning for evangelistic outreach can be done during the meeting.

Praying and planning launches team members into the harvest. Through prayer, we are empowered and guided by the Holy Spirit. This allows Christ to live out His life through the cell. In response to our prayers, the Holy Spirit will draw people to Christ through the life, witness, and ministry of the members.

Evangelism is the most uneasy portion of the Christian walk to most believers. It is the most difficult thing to do on a consistent basis. Thus, the evangelistic thrust must be overemphasized in order to maintain a proper balance in cell group life. It is almost impossible to overemphasize evangelism, but you should try.

The formal portion of the meeting should be closed with prayer.

Fellowship (10-15 minutes)
Include a time of informal fellowship either 10 minutes prior to or after the meeting. Refreshments may be served, but be careful

that the refreshments stay light and do not become a focus of your meeting. The cell servant is responsible to prevent hostess competition to serve the best refreshments.

Those who need to leave before the fellowship time should be given the opportunity to do so gracefully. Some informal fellowship should be allowed to extend beyond the 90 minutes, but there should be a predetermined cut-off point such as 15 minutes beyond the end of the scheduled time. It is very important that visitors to the cell group become the focal point of the fellowship time. If a cell group breaks down into cliches for fellowship and focuses their conversations on themselves and church, then you can be assured that the group has a real problem with carnality. There should be nothing more important to the group than its visitors (including any children). That is what Christ would do if He were there, and if you are meeting in the name of Christ, He *is* there!

Review

The cell group meeting will generally last 90 minutes. While there should be some flexibility during each meeting as to how long different parts of the meeting last, the overall time should not vary.

The host should plan for a two hour commitment. The exception to this rule is during times of extended training which will take the length of the meetings to two hours for a limited period of time. In this case, the host should plan for a two and one half hour maximum commitment.

The breakdown of your time will be something like this:

Ice Breaker ....10-15 minutes
Praise ....10-15 minutes
The Word...................................10 minutes
Edification ....30-40 minutes
Evangelism ....15-20 minutes
SUB-TOTAL ....1 1/2 hours
Fellowship.................................10-15 minutes

TOTAL ....1 hour & 45 minutes

Children

One of the most common questions regarding the cell group meeting is what to do with the children when your group includes small children. Since the cell group is an extension of the family and represents the family of God, children should not be left out. Members are in the process of becoming an extended family, i.e. the family of God. Youth, who have their own cell groups, need not attend adult meetings, but the children should be a part of it.

Children are too young to participate in such a lengthy meeting where some of the discussions would be unsuitable for them. The children may be taken into another part of the home, a nearby home, or outdoors. Caring for the children should not be thought of as just baby-sitting. The children need to have their own time of relationship building and sharing of needs and problems. Members, including the men, may take turns leading the children. This is not a burden or duty but an opportunity for the bonding of relationships between adult members of the cell group and the children. You may even consider having children refer to adult members as aunts and uncles.

If the homes of your cell group members are too small to have room for the children, and it's not appropriate for them to meet outside for weather or other reasons, then have the children meet in another nearby home while the adults meet. You may also be forced to open up the church facility for children to meet during the cell time, but this should be a last resort. If there is only one home large enough for both adults and children, you may have to meet in that home every week instead of rotating among the homes.

The children's time should begin with several songs for children followed by an opening prayer. Older children may be encouraged to assist the smaller children. Then the children should have an opportunity to share what is happening in their lives, both good and bad. Usually this will provide an opportunity for other children and the adults to bring in wise counsel and instruction from a Christian perspective. Either during or following this time, simple prayers can be offered.

A significant portion of the time can be spent in unstructured playing. Arts and crafts may be used, but usually this requires more preparation time than some of the unartistic adults may be comfortable with. Diversity in activities should be considered as positive, not negative. A Bible or missions story may be read and briefly discussed. A better way to bring in scripture is through a teachable moment. As situations arise during playing and talking about the interests or problems of the children, appropriate Bible verses may be introduced even if the adult can only paraphrase it.

The focus of the play time should be relational rather than content oriented. These relationships may be between the children and God, the children and the adult, and between the children themselves. Sometime during the meeting, very light refreshments may be provided for the children.

As the cell groups multiply, someone should take the responsibility of planning out a simple curriculum sheet for the children during the adult cell group meetings. The outline could look like this:

> •*Opening Prayer*
> •*Ice Breaker*
> •*Songs*
> •*Bible or Missions Story*
> •*Sharing and Prayer*
> •*Playtime or Planned Activity*
> •*Refreshments*
> •*Playtime*

In chapter ten, this outline is provided as a worksheet that may be photocopied for your use.

It is very important that the children understand the importance of reaching out to new children whose parents are visiting the cell group. The children should make the visitors the center of attention and make them feel loved and welcome. Children need to be regularly reminded of this. If properly taught, children will recognize this as an important avenue of their service to Christ for the purpose of evangelism to both the new children and their parents.

Cells with children should be creative in meeting the children's needs. Some churches allow children to join the adults for the ice breaker and praise time. Some include them during the Word time.

You may want to occasionally center the entire cell time around the children.

The children may join the parents during the fellowship time following the cell group meeting. Be sensitive to the needs of the children and do not extend the meetings so long that the children become unhappy and tired.

Bible Study

Another common concern about cell groups is the lack of Bible study in the cells. Although ten minutes is spent in the reading and study of scripture in the cell group, where does the study of the Bible take place in the cell church?

First of all, there should be an emphasis on the personal daily reading of scripture. This can be done church-wide by having individual members reading the same portions of scripture from week to week.

There should also be an emphasis on the reading of scripture as a family on a daily basis. This is an important time for parents to instruct their children in the Word and show the importance of the Bible in our lives. According to scripture, it is the parents who have the primary responsibility for religious education, not the church.

The next focus on scripture should be during the proclamation of the Word during the celebration time. It is important in the cell church that the preaching be based upon a verse by verse sharing of scripture. In celebration to God, we do not need to hear the opinions of men; we need to hear from God. Without this type of preaching, the cell church will be weak in its understanding of the Bible.

Finally, there may be an equipping time for church members that meets before or after the celebration time. During this time, there can be classes on Biblical instruction. These classes do not need to be organized into small groups, with the possible exception of the children. The small group structure is in the cells. Bible book studies should be offered during this time, as well as classes such as how to study the Bible, prayer, missions, etc. There are other options for Bible teaching that may be preferred or added such as independent study, retreats, week-day classes, etc.

The Cell TEAM Shares

—————— ❖ ——————

Why is it so important to have a time of praise before the group begins to minister to one another?

Should it be possible for someone to attend a cell group meeting with a serious problem and leave that meeting still hurting and with that problem still hidden from the group? How can group members work to keep such a thing from happening?

Why is it all right for visitors to hear the plans for ministry and outreach when some similar plans may be directed at that visitor? Do you think visitors will mind having group members pray for them during the meeting?

How do you think a visitor will have a better understanding of what it means to be a Christian after a cell group meeting?

What types of unbelievers are not yet ready to attend a cell group? Why? What can you do to get them ready?

7

Understanding Outsiders

❖

Responsiveness To the Gospel

Those who are outside the Christian faith can be described as either close to the kingdom or far away from the kingdom. Our approach to reach these people for Christ is very different. Many people have tried to describe ways to categorize people in terms of their responsiveness to the gospel. The different categories of responsiveness can most simply be categorized as described in this chapter.

The basic need of all outsiders is Jesus Christ. But non-Christians cannot see this need because they are dead in their trespasses and sin. They are lost and without hope in the world.

And you were dead in your trespasses and sins, in which you formerly walked according to the course of this world, according to the prince of the power of the air, of the spirit that is now working in the sons of disobedience. Among them we too all formerly lived in the lusts of our flesh, indulging the desires of the flesh

*and of the mind, and were by nature children of wrath, even as
the rest . . . remember that you were at that time separate from
Christ, excluded from the commonwealth of Israel, and strangers
to the covenants of promise, having no hope and without God in
the world. (Ephesians 2:1-3,12)*

The unbeliever has *No Hope*!

The following list offers six categories of responsiveness to the
gospel.

1. Churched Unbelievers

People who are a member of a
church but have never personally
trusted in Christ as Lord and
Savior. They equate church
membership with salvation.

2. Seekers

People whose hearts have been
prepared by the seed sown by
others and the Holy Spirit. When
presented with the claims of the
gospel, they respond.

3. Open to the Message

People who are not ready to
respond to the gospel but are
open to hearing the message of
Christ through Bible studies or
cell groups.

4. Open to the Messenger

People who are not ready to
respond or hear the direct
message of the gospel but are
open to fellowship, activities and
the friendship of committed
Christians.

5. Distorted or Unaware

People who either have a nega-
tive and distorted viewpoint of
Christians or have never heard of
Jesus Christ.

6. Hostile

People who are hostile to the
gospel and everything associated
with it.

Let's consider how to reach people for Christ in each of these
six categories.

Churched Unbelievers

Churched unbelievers are people who are members of a church yet have never personally trusted in Jesus Christ as Lord and Savior. These are people who have joined a church for the wrong reasons. Possible reasons include: making business contacts, making a spouse happy, making one's parents happy, "everyone else goes to church," or social reasons. It may have been because the individual was unduly pressured to respond to a public invitation without understanding the implications or without proper counseling and follow-up. Most of these people are baptized and may be considered strong faithful members. Some may play church on Sundays and live for Satan during the week.

This is a difficult group to reach. They are blinded to the truth and have been hardened by repeated exposure to the gospel message. They do not hear the truth and do not hear the Spirit. The key to reaching this group is prayer. Every church should pray regularly for the salvation of people from their church and from the *oikoses* of church members who fall into this category. At least once a year, an evangelistic message should be preached to people in this category.

The cell group will expose people in this category. The lack of spiritual gifts, joy, and assurance will be evident in one's life when exposed to the presence of God in the cell group meetings and in the member's lives. Those in the cell group with the gift of discernment should be able to quietly and prayerfully expose people in this category.

We must also try to reach people in our personal *oikos* who are members of other churches, yet are walking in darkness. This is not stealing sheep from other churches. If we feel led of the Spirit that they are probably unbelievers, then we should pray regularly for them, expose them to Christ in us, and pray for opportunities to discuss their spiritual life so we can explain the difference between church membership and personal faith. If they are not regularly attending their church, we should also expose them to our cell groups. Once the individual is converted, we should encourage them to return to their own church if it is a Bible believing evangelical church. If they feel led of God to join your church, they should be lovingly brought into the fellowship.

Seekers

Seekers are people who are ready to respond to the good news of Jesus Christ. They are ripe for harvesting. When they clearly understand the plan of salvation, they respond by trusting in Jesus Christ as their Lord and Savior. Children of church members should fall into this category. Some of those in this group were at one time less responsive to the gospel. Through prayer and the sowing of the seed of the gospel by various people, they are ready to respond at this point.

People in this category can be reached through both direct and indirect evangelistic strategies. Direct strategies include personal visits to these individuals where the gospel is presented, and they are persuaded to accept Christ.

Indirect strategies include inviting a seeker to an evangelistic rally or crusade, giving them a Bible, tract, video, cassette, or book that clearly presents the claims of Christ. The film *Jesus* by Campus Crusade is one such example.

Of all the categories, this category is usually the smallest in terms of the number of people in a community. And yet, traditional churches expend almost all of their evangelistic resources on this group.

Open to the Message

People in this category are not yet ready to make a decision for Christ. They know something about Christ and the Christian faith, but they do not fully understand what it means to follow Christ and are not yet ready to make a commitment. Yet, they are open to learning more about Christ and are willing to associate with and relate to Christians.

People in this group are willing to attend evangelistic Bible studies and cell group meetings. They might be willing to attend church services, but they should be channeled through the cell groups rather than the church celebration services. In cell churches, the celebration time is directed toward believers, not unbelievers. It is during the intimacy of the cell group meetings that these people can come to understand what it means to follow

Christ. When unbelievers are channeled into the church through celebration times, it is easy for them to equate salvation with attending church services. Those who just attend the celebration time are usually consumer oriented and desire to remain anonymous. This often creates churched unbelievers or carnal believers who have little understanding of the costs and real joys of the Christian life.

People in this category may also be invited to an evangelistic rally or crusade, given a Bible, tract, video, cassette, or book that clearly presents the claims of Christ, or shown a film. They should not be expected to make an immediate decision. The seed is being sown for a later harvest.

This category is usually the second smallest category in terms of the number of people, although this varies a great deal from one community or country to another.

Open to the Messenger

People in this category are not ready or willing to attend Bible studies or any event that takes place at a church building. They are most open to personal relationships with committed Christians as long as they are not unduly pressed about religious things and are allowed to "be themselves."

In this group, people are primarily reached through building individual relationships with believers who pray regularly for them, let the light and joy of Christ shine through their lives, and gently point them toward Christ through the leadership of the Holy Spirit. When a need arises in this person's life, they are very open to let believers minister to them in the name of Christ.

Those open to the messenger are often willing to attend gatherings with other Christians, as long as it isn't at church and they aren't pressured to make an immediate decision for Christ. Some people in this category may attend a cell group in a person's home but will likely not become a regular attender at first. They will often attend gatherings that interest them when they are brought by a believer whom they trust as long as it is not held at a church facility. Such gatherings might include seminars on parenting, marriage enrichment, gardening, or any other topic of interest to that particular person. They are willing participants in sports and other activities with believers, but it is the individual relationships, not the activities, that will draw them to Christ.

Another ministry to this group is share groups. Share groups are informal gatherings of believers and unbelievers that meet for ten weeks. They are designed to create a non-threatening environment where people can fellowship together and share problems and ideas in such a way as to allow a Christian perspective to come through. After attending a share group for ten weeks, some will be ready to attend the cell group meeting. Share groups are discussed more fully in the next chapter.

The evangelistic objective with those in this category is to move them to the next category which will place them into a cell group or evangelistic Bible study.

The number of people in this category is often similar in size to those open to the message, although it may be a larger group.

Distorted or Unaware

People in this category are not open to the message or the messenger. They are not hostile, but neither are they friendly. Their image of Christianity is negative. They have already formed their basic philosophy of life and are generally satisfied with that philosophy. Their understanding of Christianity is either distorted, or there is no knowledge of Christianity at all.

These people are not easily reached. What they see concerning your witness is viewed through eyes and ears that are distorted both by Satan and through their past experiences and culture.

First of all, they are blinded by the evil one.

And even if our gospel is veiled, it is veiled to those who are perishing, in whose case the god of this world has blinded the minds of the unbelieving, that they might not see the light of the gospel of the glory of Christ, who is the image of God. (2 Corinthians 4:3-4)

This problem is overcome through prayer as discussed in chapter three about the power behind the cells. Another problem in reaching people who have a distorted view of the gospel is the unbeliever's frame of reference. This is an important term to grasp.

We must understand that people in the distorted category don't see things the way we see them. The same words or ideas have different meanings to them. The same objects are not perceived the same way. To understand the principle of people seeing the same thing, yet perceiving or understanding it differently, complete the following exercises.

How many squares do you see?

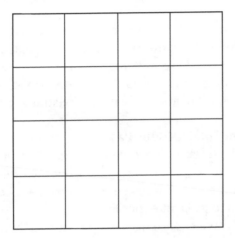

There are 9 dots in the illustration below. Take a pen or pencil and connect all 9 dots in the square using 4 straight lines. Do not lift the pen or pencil from the paper and don't retrace any line.

Your answer to the first exercise will vary from person to person. It depends on how you look at things, i.e. your frame of reference. Some people will see one square, others sixteen, and some up to 30. Many people cannot work the 9 dot puzzle because of their frame of reference. We expect that the puzzle has to be solved within the square created by the outer dots. Unless your line goes outside of this artificial boundary, forming a large triangle, you cannot solve the puzzle. An unbeliever in the distorted category has distorted expectations about life, such that they cannot see or understand things that seem so obvious and clear to us.

The term frame of reference refers to the way we perceive things. Our individual frame of reference is created by the sum total of our past experiences. Before we can witness to an unbeliever, we must understand their past experiences and the way those experiences have distorted their understanding of Christianity.

We Are The Sum Total Of Our Past!

The moment we experience something, it becomes a part of our lives, stored up as past experience. This includes every thing we do, see, hear, or feel. Past experiences cause us to respond in predictable ways to present experience.

The more positive experiences we provide to those who have a distorted view of the gospel, the more likely we will add new experiences that will challenge, balance out, and ultimately change the distorted ones.

You must establish a right to relationship (refer to pages 79-81) with people in this category and spend time with them. Find out what they enjoy doing, and go do it with them. If they enjoy camping, eating out, cooking out, skiing, fishing, or sporting events, choose one you both enjoy and do it with them.

Exposure of unbelievers to our Christian life and activity is an important factor in leading them to Christ (2 Corinthians 3:3). Much of this is done through intentional lifestyle evangelism. This means we conspicuously live out our joyful and abundant Christian life before specific individuals we have targeted for the gospel through the guidance of the Holy Spirit. We pray for them, we associate with them, we love them, we minister to their needs, and wait for Spirit sourced opportunities to share Christ in indirect and non-threatening ways. The directness of that witness will increase over time.

In 1980, I spent two weeks studying Yoido Full Gospel Church in Seoul, Korea. The pastor of this largest church in the world (700,000 members), David Yonggi Cho, said the foundation of their evangelistic strategy was simple. He said cell group members would walk the narrow streets near their homes looking for people who showed signs of stress in their eyes. The cell member would begin walking along side of this distressed person and begin a conversation. They would attempt to discover the reason for the stress in that person's life. If they were able to discover the problem, they considered that person caught in the web. The entire cell group (or church if need be) would do everything within their power to solve the problem and minister to that person and their family in love. With all the prayer, love, and ministry directed toward that person, it was unlikely that they could escape without coming to Christ.

If you can discover the problems of the people in your *oikos*, even those in this distorted category, the entire cell can focus on loving and ministering to that person and their family in the name of Christ. While we minister on an earthly level, our main battle is waged in the heavenlies through prayer. Through your ministry and prayers, this individual may truly come to know the love of Christ, have a wonderful opportunity to understand the undistorted truth of Christ, and have an opportunity to respond and accept Christ as their personal Savior.

Most of those who are completely unaware of Christ must be approached as if they had a distorted image of Christ. It is possible that those who are unaware will respond more quickly than those whose views are distorted. Many of those who are unaware of Christ are living in a culture that is foreign to Christianity.

In some communities, this category will be the largest category in terms of the percentage of unbelievers.

Hostile

This category is the same as the previous one, with one major exception: hostility. The basic underlying principles are the same as in the previous category, except each obstacle is larger and more difficult to overcome. The amount of prayer must be intensified since the opposition of the evil one is greater. If they know you are a Christian, they will dislike you and be very wary of you. Reaching them will take time and require patience. A lot of time will be spent in building trust with little or no discussion of spiritual things. Opportunities for ministry will be vital, yet results will come slowly and require much follow up.

The size of this group in the community varies greatly from country to country and sub-culture to sub-culture.

The Cell TEAM Shares
❖

Discuss the term frame of reference. If anyone in the group had to change their frame of reference before their conversion, ask them to share a brief testimony about how this was accomplished in their lives.

The problem of the dots is solved as follows:

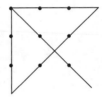

As a group, select one person from the *oikoses* of group members that represents each of the 6 categories. Ask the person who knows this individual to describe why this person belongs to a certain category of responsiveness to the gospel. Discuss possible approaches to reaching each selected person for Christ.

8

Reaching People Through Cells

❖

We have already discussed several aspects of evangelism through cell groups. We have considered the role of prayer in providing the power behind our evangelistic efforts. We have looked at the importance of *oikos* relationships as a channel for our evangelistic activities. We have also considered responsiveness to the gospel as a determinant in choosing our evangelistic strategy. Now we need to bring all of these principles together to help individual cell members, cell groups, and your church work together in bringing the gospel to the unchurched and unsaved in your community.

Before you can design a strategy, you must first understand your community and focus your strategies on specific groups of people within your community. Once you have decided who you intend to reach, your church must design specific strategies to reach the selected group(s) of people. In this chapter, individual cell group members will learn how to design their own strategy to reach those in their *oikos* and to penetrate the *oikoses* of others. Then ideas are suggest to help the cell group design its group strategy to help one another in their evangelistic thrust. The chapter then presents ways the church can use its combined resources to assist the cells in reaching the unchurched.

Understanding Your Community

Before you can reach your community for Christ you must understand, as much as possible, the demographics of your community. You must understand the way your community and your church is broken down into such things as race, economic status, occupations, culture, religion, and age. People are most effective in reaching others for Christ who come from similar socio-economic backgrounds. Your church should have already conducted some research to answer most of the first three questions. If so, get a copy of the findings and take some time to carefully answer these and the two questions which follow.

1. Based upon your church's research and/or upon your own personal observations, in what ways are your church and community alike? (race, income, education, values, occupations, age, etc.)

2. In what ways are they different?

3. Which specific socio-economic groups of people does your church feel led to target for Christ?

4. Look for *rights to relationship* that will open doors to building relationships with those who are unchurched in your area. What sports, leisure activities, or hobbies do the people you intend to evangelize enjoy?

5. What are the problems, hurts, needs, and stresses that people in your target group are experiencing?

Designing Your Personal Strategy

Unbelievers

Your own strategy for reaching the unchurched will be built around people who are in your personal, extended, and potential *oikos*. In order to help you visualize this, complete the following exercises. Later, you should complete this exercise on each person in your *oikos*.

In the space below, list six people from your own *oikos* (see page 77). [i.e. your wife, your next door neighbor, etc.]

List two people who are in the *oikoses* of those in your *oikos* (your extended *oikos*). [i.e. your wife's boss and your wife's best friend.]

1. _____

   1. _____

   2. _____

2. _____

   1. _____

   2. _____

3. _____

   1. _____

   2. _____

4. _____

   1. _____

   2. _____

5. _____   1. _____

                                2. _____

6. _____   1. _____

                                2. _____

1. Circle the people who are not active church members from the previous list.

2. Now list skills, talents, and areas of interest in your own life that would give you a *right to relationship* with others in your community (see pages 79-81). This is your potential *oikos*.

3. List ways in which your spiritual gifts might be used to reach people for Christ in your personal, extended, or potential *oikos*.

4. List your neighbors who are not active church members. (If you do not know many of your neighbors, getting to know them should be one of the first parts of your personal strategy.)

5. What are some things you could do to build a relationship and minister to a new neighbor?

6. Those who are unchurched from your *oikos* and from your extended *oikos* form the core group of people you need to target for Christ. Prayerfully select 3 to 5 people from this group to target for Christ. Write their names below.

If you do not know many unchurched people from these categories, you will need to discover a man or woman of peace from your potential *oikos* relationships (refer to page 81 for a review).

7. What *rights to relationship* listed on the previous page from your potential *oikos* will you use to find unchurched people to target for the gospel?

8. Now select one person who is unchurched and probably an unbeliever to design a sample strategy that could be used to reach them for Christ. Write their name below.

9. Which of the 6 categories of responsiveness would you think this person belongs to?

10. Describe your strategy of prayer for reaching this person.

11. How can you change your daily actions, attitudes, and lifestyle to be a more effective witness?

12. What can you do to spend more quality time to build a closer relationship with this person?

13. Depending on their responsiveness, what approach would be best to introduce them to the gospel? (Review Chapter 7 if necessary.)

NOTE: Although it is beyond the scope of this book, in order to bring people to Christ, you must know how to give your personal testimony, respond to questions about your faith, and lead someone to understand the plan of salvation and pray to accept Jesus Christ as their personal Lord and Savior. There are many acceptable ways to learn this.

Unchurched Believers

There may be many people in your community who are unchurched believers. These people accepted Christ at some point in the past, but have either drifted away from Christ or have been driven away. Many of these people have been turned off, hurt, or burned out by past church experience and have rejected the church while not rejecting the person of Christ. These people are often drawn to the intimacy and spiritual depth of the cell church. Pray for them and invite them to your cell groups. Show them what the family of God can be like.

Others in this category have drifted away from God and have become carnal. Pray for these people and ask God to bring circumstances into their lives to draw them back to Himself. Often these prayers will result in crises in the person's life. When the crises come, be prepared to minister and draw them back to God. Bring them directly into the cell group so they can experience spiritual and emotional healing. Seek a recommitment of their lives to God. Disciple and involve them in prayer and evangelism.

Your Cell Group Strategy

Many of the activities needed to bring people to Christ are difficult for individuals to do on their own. Here's where the cell group can assist individual members in reaching people for Christ.

First of all, the cell group can provide an expanded prayer base to reach people for Christ. Each week during the cell meeting, and on a daily basis, cell group members can pray for one another's witness.

Cell group servants and members can also assist one another in designing a strategy for each person and trouble shooting with one another as those strategies are worked out.

Cell members can work together in areas where their strategies overlap and form a share group, evangelistic Bible study, friendship group or ministry strategy. Since most cell groups will have a general geographic area where their members live, they can also minister to new families moving into their area.

New Families

Moving into a new town or neighborhood is a traumatic experience for most families. Old relationships are broken, and a world of familiarity suddenly becomes a world of unknowns. If cell group members are alert and keep an eye on homes that are for sale, the cell group can be ready for action shortly after the moving van arrives. Whenever a new neighbor comes into a community, the cell group can welcome and help them make adjustments.

Discover their needs and welcome them not just with words, but through ministry. Regardless of where they are in terms of responsiveness to the gospel, if you minister to them as they arrive in the community, and they accept your ministry, you will establish a *right to relationship* that will lay the groundwork for reaching this family for Christ. If they are already believers, they may be open to becoming a part of your fellowship. If your ministry is done in the name of Christ, even if there is no visible response to your ministry, your efforts are not in vain and will be rewarded.

Evangelistic Bible Study

If there are two or more people in your cell group who have unchurched friends who are *open to the message*, then join together and conduct an evangelistic Bible study. Often the only way to find out if people will attend such a study is to ask them. Very often people are surprised at how many friends will attend an informal Bible study conducted away from a church building. If you center your study on a topic of interest to the group, they are more likely to attend. Serendipity has a series of evangelistic Bible studies for youth, one for baby boomers in the U.S.A., and a Bible book series. You may also build a Bible study around the showing of the *Jesus* film by Campus Crusade.

The Bible study should have a predetermined length such as 6 to 12 weeks. A good ratio of believers and unbelievers is about 1 believer to 3 unbelievers. The maximum size of the group should be 15, but 8 to 12 is more manageable. Once the Bible study has been completed, encourage unbelievers who attended to visit your cell group.

Share Groups

If two to four people in your cell group have people in their *oikos* who may be *open to the messenger,* start a share group. This is for people who are not open to attending a church function and not necessarily open to directly studying the message through a Bible study. They would, however, come together in an informal gathering of believers and unbelievers to share and discuss relevant issues in their lives. These discussions will give Christian members an opportunity to share a Christian response to issues discussed.

A share group has a predetermined length of ten weeks. Ideally, it moves between members' homes to give an opportunity for group members to really get to know one another. You can start a share group by personally inviting neighbors or others in your *oikos* to join your ten-week group. Each of the cell group members should invite two to three unbelievers. The ideal size is 8 to 10. The absolute maximum is 12. The whole dynamic of the share group will break down in any group larger than 12. Explain to the unbelievers exactly what you intend to do, and encourage them to come for the fellowship and interaction. You may be surprised how many people will come.

The share group is designed to create a non-threatening environment where people can fellowship together and share problems and ideas in such a way as to allow a Christian perspective to come through. It's something like a water downed version of a cell group with a greater emphasis upon fellowship and relationships.

The initial share group will be centered around an ice breaker and getting to know one another. At this meeting, you will also plan what the group will do. Break into small groups composed of each believer and their guests. Each group will choose the topics for their proportion of the remaining meetings. Topics will include areas of interest to the group. These might include such topics as how to deal with stress at work, making your children feel secure and loved, why is there so much suffering in the world, or almost any other topic of interest to your group. It may include global events or issues, but generally it is wise to stay away from political or other issues which may generate heated arguments. Each group will lead the sessions in which they chose the topic. Allow unbelievers to have some ownership and facilitate a group meeting if they desire to do so.

The length of the meeting should be between 60 to 90 minutes. It is good to serve light refreshments at the beginning of the meeting. Children should be handled in a way similar to the cell group meeting.

The share group would begin with an ice breaker, then have a brief introduction to the topic by the group in charge, followed by discussions of issues relevant to the lives of non-Christian group members. The Christian perspective is shared in a non-judgmental way. The group must listen to opposing non-Christian views without confrontation. These opposing views give an opportunity to clarify and explain the differences between what the Bible teaches and what non-Christians in your culture believe. The group will support one another and attempt to minister to one another. Christian members can use their spiritual gifts to minister to the non-Christians.

A low-key prayer time may or may not be conducted, with non-Christians not expected to participate. Any prayer time should be very brief at the first few sessions and slowly expand as the group begins to trust one another. After attending a share group for ten weeks, some may be ready to attend a Bible study or the cell group meeting. Others will take more time through developing personal relationships and trust before they can be brought a step closer to the gospel. If the group wants to continue meeting as a share group, do so for another ten week period, but do not extend the share group as an on-going extended event. Channel those who want to continue meeting into the cell group.

Friendship or Focus Groups

If there are two or more people in your cell group who have people in their *oikos* with a *distorted* view of the gospel, then start a friendship group. A friendship group is a six to eight week gathering of people usually from your extended or potential *oikos*. Its sole purpose is to establish a *right to relationship* with people.

The friendship group will target a group of people using a topic of interest to draw them together. Topics can include such things as gardening, arts and crafts, sports, computer programming, interior decorating, weight loss, nutrition, tax preparation, playing the guitar, financial planning, aerobics, etc.

It is important that the person leading the session has expertise or credentials on that topic. People will feel cheated if they come to a study group on something they know as much about as the facilitator. Select people from your church who have expertise in a given area and ask them to assist you. Potential leaders may include doctors, nurses, nutritionists, accountants, lawyers, coaches, financial planners, etc. You may even invite an expert who is not from your church to lead the group.

The meetings should last about one hour to a maximum of 90 minutes. The lesson plan should be easy to develop if the leader has expertise on the topic. Allow plenty of time for fellowship following each meeting. This is the primary purpose of the meeting. Try to establish a personal relationship with unchurched group members outside of the friendship group meetings. You may want to follow-up your friendship group with a share feast as described later in this chapter. Bring someone from your friendship group into your *oikos* if possible. Begin praying for each person and begin the process of moving them to the point where they are *open to the messenger*.

Ministry Strategy

Regardless of the responsiveness of the person you are trying to reach, opportunities for ministry will arise that go beyond your ability as an individual to meet. Bring these opportunities to your cell group. Work together to provide for that need. If need be, call upon the resources of the church to assist. But whatever you do, remember these two things:

1. Do it so that the ministry provides an opportunity to deepen the personal relationship between the cell group member and the person receiving the ministry. The ministry should not be perceived as coming from the church. To many people, the church is no different than a government relief agency. Social services are taken for granted as a right, with no sense of appreciation or gratitude. The cell church ministry should be perceived as coming from an individual(s) who loves them and cares for them for the express purpose of eventually bringing them to faith in Christ.

2. This ministry should be done in the name of Christ. Many people may wonder about your motives. Few people give of themselves without expecting something in return. We love others and minister to them as an expression of Christ's love. We cannot change their attitudes about Christ and His followers if our ministry is not done in His name.

Share Feasts

Another ministry of your cell group should be share feasts. Share feasts are cell group cook-outs, dinners, or parties. Sometimes your share feast should include just cell group members and visitors to the cell group. This creates an opportunity for good fellowship with one another and gives a chance for cell group visitors to deepen relationships and experience the joy of the Christian life and community.

At other share feasts, you should invite the people you are trying to reach for the gospel who are not ready to attend a regular cell group meeting. You may or may not want to have planned games and activities as long as everyone has a good time. You might have a brief time of sharing, but nothing preachy, and no devotionals or Bible studies.

Prayer

The cell group can assist one another in their personal efforts of evangelism by praying for one another and their witness by name and specific circumstances. This should be done at cell group meetings and on a personal daily intercessory level.

Conclusion to Cell Strategies

Whichever strategies are chosen, one of the basic objectives is to draw people into your cell group. This may occur before or after their personal commitment to Christ. Often it will occur before their conversion. Once they are converted, the person who leads them to the Lord should begin a period of one-on-one discipleship. Bring them to the celebration time and enroll them in the next new member's class. Included in their discipleship should be the process of trying to reach the people in their *oikos* for Christ.

Your Church's Supporting Strategies

Some of the activities needed to bring people to Christ are difficult for either an individual or a cell group to do on their own. In this case, the church can assist individual members and cell groups in reaching people for Christ through a variety of supporting strategies.

Ministry Pool

Often there is a ministry need to an individual or family that goes beyond the resources of individuals or cell groups. Professionals in your church should pool their resources by donating a certain percentage of their time (weekly or monthly) to use their skills to minister to people in need. Doctors, lawyers, psychologists, accountants, bankers, builders, and businessmen can all provide services. For instance, if a person has lost their job and are about to lose their home, the ministry pool can assist them in getting employment and advise them on their finances with strategies that can help save their home.

Evangelistic Events

When a church has been actively doing the work of evangelism and is ready for a harvest, the church can conduct a one or two evening evangelistic rally. Depending on the context, this rally may be at the church facilities or at a neutral site. Its purpose would be to bring in the harvest from the seed sown through the ministry of church members and the cell groups.

Other events may revolve around Christmas or Easter. Evangelistic Bible studies might be offered throughout a community in preparation for Easter, culminating in a special evangelistic service where the plan of salvation is clearly presented. Around Christmas, church members can conduct an open house in each of their homes for fellowship and the reading of the Christmas story. This could cover a significant number of people in an entire community.

Retreats

The church can offer various retreats to give individual church members an opportunity to invite unchurched friends to a special setting. This, in effect, draws unchurched people away from the world and brings them into the Christian fellowship of believers. Youth retreats are common, but why not marriage enrichment retreats for young couples? Weekend retreats and outings for senior citizens also have much potential for evangelism. Father/son fishing trips or tournaments could be held. The only limitation is the types of interests among the unchurched in your community.

Seminars

The church should also plan seminars or banquets that would bring in outstanding speakers on topics of interest to the unchurched. These events will give an opportunity to present the Christian perspective. Topics might include child rearing, stress management, weight loss, etc. Why not have a sports (i.e. basketball) clinic, and bring in a well known collegiate or professional athlete or coach.

Consider bringing in a well-known entertainer who would be willing to give a personal testimony. Hold a banquet at a hotel; bring in people through your church's *oikos*; serve a quality meal; have a time of entertainment followed by a personal testimony.

Context Specific Ministries

A variety of ministries should be offered by the church to provide an opportunity for individual members to build relationships with the unchurched. These should be designed around the interests and needs of the specific community.

Ministry to children might include backyard Bible clubs, an afternoon program for latch-key kids, or a day care program for either preschool or the elderly. A sports league might be established for all ages but should be used for building relationships rather than requiring church attendance.

Other context specific ministries might include such things as the provision of meals or groceries, job training, education, or community development programs. The guidelines for ministry through the church are similar to those listed about the cell group on pages 119 and 120. Make sure that the ministry provides an opportunity to deepen the personal relationship between a church (cell group) member and the person receiving the ministry.

Training

The church must support this infrastructure of evangelism and ministry with adequate training. Much of this will be done through the cell groups, but some of it will require specific training for specific ministries set up by the church. Do not require your people to come to church at another time during the week. Conduct your training either before or after your worship time. In addition to Bible study classes, offer training in prayer, spiritual warfare, and witnessing.

Overview

In order to conceptualize the overall picture of evangelism in a cell church, review the Cell Church Evangelistic Flow Chart on the next page. There are four stages to evangelism in a cell church.

The first stage is cultivation. All cell group members must be personally involved in prayer for the evangelistic activities of each person in the cell group. The evangelistic outreach of the cell group will not advance beyond the prayer of the cell members. Each cell member must also be consistently involved in building bridges of relationship with those in their *oikos* through lifestyle evangelism.

The second stage is sowing. Both cell group and church-wide activities should bring unbelievers into seed sowing activities that are designed for people from each level of receptiveness to the gospel.

The third stage is reaping the harvest. This takes place primarily through the cell groups. People whose lives are touched through the sowing activities should be channeled into the cell groups. Some will make a decision for Christ before they enter the cell group, but many will enter the cell group before their conversion. Once they experience the power of God and the ministry of the Holy Spirit in the cells, many will choose to accept Christ as their personal Lord and Savior.

As the Lord leads, and if there is a harvest to be gathered, then the church may choose to conduct an evangelistic rally in a neutral site away from the church facility. Cell group members may bring those who are ready for the harvest to such an event. Those who accept Christ should be channeled back into the cell group either

Cell Church Evangelistic Flow Chart

Stage IV	Stage III	Stage II	Stage I
Reproduction	Reaping	Sowing	Cultivation

Discipleship
which begins
the cycle
of evangelism
again with
new believers

Cell Groups

Rallies

Share Groups

Ministry/Focus
Groups

Evangelistic
Bible Studies

Seminars

Special Events

Recreation
Ministry

Prayer

Lifestyle
Evangelism

through the individual who sowed the seed for the harvest or by assigning each convert to an appropriate cell group.

The final stage is extremely important. New believers must be brought into the fellowship of the body to worship and experience God. They must be discipled and thrust immediately into service. A primary part of their discipleship and service will be for the new believer to begin to reach out to unbelievers in their *oikos*. Their new found joy and enthusiasm will draw others to Jesus Christ.

The Cell TEAM Shares
❖

Discuss the specific socio-economic groups of people your church is especially trying to reach in your community.

Ask team members to share their personal strategies to reach those in their *oikos* for Christ.

How can you bring more unchurched people into your *oikos*?

Which group strategies might your cell group use to reach people for Christ? Which team members might work together using which group strategies?

What supporting strategies from your church would best assist your cell group in evangelism?

Review the evangelistic flow chart. Name people you know that are at each of the four stages.

Section Four

Leading
a Cell Group

9

Cell Group
Servants

❖

Servants, Not Leaders

In the secular world, leadership is equated with power and prestige. Those who are placed into leadership positions are done so because they are supposedly the most gifted and capable people who are able to lead and direct others. But as Jesus indicated to His disciples, it is not this way among His followers.

And there arose also a dispute among them as to which one of them was regarded to be greatest. And He said to them, "The kings of the Gentiles lord it over them; and those who have authority over them are called 'Benefactors.' But not so with you, but let him who is the greatest among you become as the youngest, and the leader as the servant. For who is greater, the one who reclines at the table, or the one who serves? Is it not the one who reclines at the table? But I am among you as the one who serves." (Luke 22:24-27)

An organizational chart for the cell group would look like this from a secular perspective:

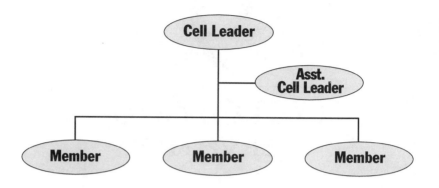

In reality, however, the cell group organizational chart must be turned right side up.

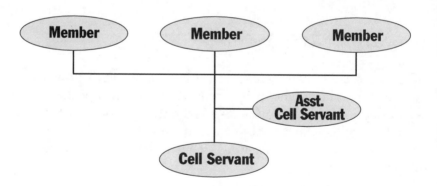

The cell servant lifts up and supports those whom they have been given the responsibility to serve.

Jesus Himself gave us the example of the leader as servant. He gave His life in service to others. In fact, this concept was so important to Jesus, he directly instructed us not to be called leaders so that there would never be any question about the difference between secular leadership and Christian servant-hood.

And do not be called leaders; for one is your leader, that is, Christ. But the greatest among you shall be your servant. And whoever exalts himself shall be humbled; and whoever humbles himself shall be exalted. (Matthew 23:10-12)

Those who lead the cell groups are to be called servants, not leaders. This is not just a matter of semantics. The cell group servants are to humble themselves and model the Christian life by serving others. The leader of each cell group is Jesus Christ. Christ directs the cell group team through the Holy Spirit.

And so when He had washed their feet, and taken His garments, and reclined at the table again, He said to them, "Do you know what I have done to you? You call me Teacher and Lord; and you are right, for so I am. If I then, the Lord and the Teacher, washed your feet, you also ought to wash one another's feet. For I gave you an example that you also should do as I did to you." (John 13:12-15)

As a cell group servant, you do not just tell other people what to do, *you show them.* Take others along with you as you serve so that they may imitate you, as you allow Christ to live out His life through you (Galatians 2:20).

Small Group Dynamics

To adequately serve a small group, you must understand some basic principles of how small groups work. History is a record of small group accomplishments. When people join together in small groups for an important task, things begin to happen. It's almost as if a new organism has been created. The group begins to grow and mature and becomes something greater and more effective than just the sum of the people who make up the group.

Although cell groups are theocratic (governed by God) and are under the authority of the whole body (the church), it is through the democratic process that we come to an understanding of what God wants the group to do. As long as group members are living under the lordship of Christ, the Holy Spirit can show the group how God intends for the group to accomplish its task.

Study the following picture story carefully. It illustrates some of the principles of democratic group leadership.

In your own words, write a short story about the cartoon on the previous page. Refer back to the cartoon as you write. The story should begin, "Once upon a time," and there should be a moral to the story at the conclusion. Demonstrate the basic principles of small group leadership as portrayed in the illustrations.

There are many leadership models a small group can follow, but cell groups should follow the democratic model. This model emphasizes the cell servant as an enabler. The *enabler* is one who plays the servant role as Christ taught with the basin and towel (John 13). This model creates a climate conducive to high levels of motivation and results. It increases the potential for group members to discover their own needs as well as the needs of others. It also increases the motivation of group members because there is a sense of joint ownership.

Motivation

One of the keys to leading a cell group is motivating people. Many people try to motivate others through external gimmicks, but true motivation to serve comes from within individuals in response to their own met needs and the desire to meet the needs of others. It is our physical, emotional, and spiritual needs that motivate us. If you are meeting the needs of your group members, they will be motivated to serve.

Let's look at four keys to motivating a cell group:
1. Cell group members are motivated by the Holy Spirit. If members and servants are praying for one another, the Holy Spirit will be the primary source for the motivation of the group.

2. Cell members are motivated when they are challenged with the great importance of the cell's task. When the biblical imperative for reaching others for Christ is laid before the group, and they realize they can really do something about it, the task of evangelism can rally the group to action. As people are won to Christ, the motivation increases.

3. Cell members are motivated when they feel a part of a team effort with a worthwhile goal. With accountability to the group and the support of one another, the group can accomplish its task. As the team develops an appreciation and love for one another, the team becomes family.

4. Cell members are motivated when their self-worth is affirmed and enhanced. Through weekly affirmation and encouragement, the group task becomes a joy and a mission. Affirmation comes through the acceptance and respect of group members. Affirmation is demonstrated by trusting group members with delegated responsibilities. Affirmation also comes through both public and private praise and encouragement for a job well done or a good effort given.

The group process is powerful, but it only works when the group has a task, a mission, and a way to accomplish that task. Small groups with no other purpose than to learn or study do not have the same powerful dynamic.

Small Group Leadership Skills

Listening
An important skill in leading small groups is listening. Usually we only listen to what we want to hear. As a cell group servant, we should listen to see the world from the other's point of view as

much as possible. We should also listen under the leadership of the Holy Spirit so He can reveal things to us that we would otherwise overlook. Thus our purpose in listening is to understand not only what the person says, but what the person means and how the person feels. If we are a good listener, we can use the information we hear to know how to minister to people and to help them understand themselves and the importance of their relationship with God. Such listening helps to create a non-threatening environment and improves personal relationships in the group. It requires patience and practice but is an important skill to develop.

Observation

To open up our internal attitudes and feelings, we must literally open up the external arrangements. We should sit in a circle of chairs (or on the floor), facing one another, with nothing to hide behind such as a table. An informal environment, such as a living room or den, is ideal. This allows everyone to see one another verbally and non-verbally. Eye contact and body language are a large part of our communication of feelings to one another. Can you identify the meaning of the following non-verbal signals?

    shy   _____   _____   _____

This exercise may seem simple. Often these signals are quite clear yet we seldom notice them or address the problem if we do notice them.

Clarification

Many times there is a difference between what an individual means to say and what we hear them say. A cell group servant should be a good listener and help team members clarify what they mean during a time of sharing or discussion. This is most simply done by restating what the other person has said, but in your own words. When we mix Christians and non-Christians together, we have a group of people with many different backgrounds, frame of references, and terminologies. If the person agrees with your restatement, then you have probably communicated. If not, the other person should restate their phrase in another way.

Modeling

As a cell servant, what you *do* has more impact than what you *say*!

What you *do*, not what you *say*, tells others what you really believe. Whatever you want your team members to do, you must not only explain it to them, you must show them. This is called *modeling*. If you want your group members to be relaxed and informal in the group, then you must be relaxed and informal. If you want them to share openly, then you must share openly from your own life. If you want them to reach out and bring people to the cell group meeting, then you must take the lead and bring someone new to the group.

When my son was six months old, we wanted to teach him to wave good-bye to people. There was no way we could communicate with him through words, so if someone was leaving our home, we waved our hands so he could see us. Soon, whenever we waved good-bye, he waved good-bye too. This pattern of modeling follows us throughout our lives. Paul told the Corinthians to imitate him as he imitated Christ. Christ taught as much through His lifestyle as He did through His parables.

Stay on Target

The group process is enhanced when the group has a specific and significant goal. In order to develop a team spirit, there must be something important to work toward. A soccer team works together to win a game. The objective of the team is to score more goals than the other team. The team develops teamwork through practicing together. In the beginning, the team has trouble working together and is ineffective. As the individuals learn to work together, the team will produce a greater corporate effort and win more games.

In the cell group, there is no higher purpose than winning people to Christ. The other purposes of the cell group such as worship, caring, fellowship, and ministering come more naturally. Sharing Christ is one of the most threatening and difficult things we do and is against our human nature.

In the beginning, the group will probably not be very effective in their evangelistic efforts. But as the cell group begins to work together for a common cause, it will learn the most effective ways to achieve its purpose. The members should always be aware of the group's evangelistic goals and work toward them. If the cell group loses sight of its evangelistic purpose, it will become just another activity or meeting. When this happens, the cell group will begin to decline.

Holy Spirit

Cell group servants must be filled with the Holy Spirit and be sensitive to His leadership. They must know their spiritual gifts and exercise them. It is best if they have at least one of the servant gifts (leadership, administration, encouragement, prophecy, or teaching). They should lead group members to discover and exercise their own spiritual gifts. The cell servant must allow the Holy Spirit to direct and lead the cell group's ministry as well as its meetings. The Holy Spirit leads in a powerful, orderly, consistent, and doctrinally sound manner.

The cell servant must be a person of prayer. They should model prayer both in their personal lives, with group members, and during the meeting. Their prayers should not be showy or preachy, but sincere and natural. The servant should prepare for each meeting through prayer. The cell group will not likely have more spiritual power available to it than the prayer life of its servant will allow.

Toward Group Maturity

Why is it so important to study small group leadership? Because any new group begins as relatively immature, with most individuals being primarily interested in themselves. Often people will misunderstand what others are saying. Conflicts will arise and motivation will drop. A servant who understands the group process and has good communication skills can help lead the group toward maturity. A mature group has learned to be other centered and is more motivated to accomplish the goals of the group. The mature group has learned how to dialogue so they can better understand one another. Thus interpersonal relationships are improved, and the bond of love between group members increases.

There is much power in the group process. The cell group, however, has even greater potential because the Holy Spirit, who leads each one of our lives, is *one* Spirit. It is through Him that we become *one*. Through prayer, we become intercessors and partners with the Holy Spirit in proclaiming Jesus Christ and leading people to the foot of the cross.

The Cell TEAM Shares
❖

Why are those who lead the cell groups called servants rather than leaders?

Share the stories written about the democratic group process. What principles of leadership are illustrated? What are their implications for the cell group?

Discuss the small group leadership skills. Are these just for the cell servants, or can group members use these skills as well?

What does it take for a new cell group to become a mature group? How will this affect your life?

10

Administration

❖

Structure

For the cell group ministry to run smoothly, it must be properly organized. The cell groups are the foundational ministry of the church. Everything else revolves around the cells.

The head of the church is Jesus Christ, and the final authority for what the church does should be from the Word. Church decisions are made by the corporate body of Christ under the leadership of the Holy Spirit. The senior pastor must be the overseer and shepherd of the body using a servant model of leadership. The senior pastor is responsible for directing the ministry of the cell groups. Some of the responsibility will be delegated, but the ministry will not realize its potential unless the pastor is the spiritual and motivational leader of the cell groups.

The chart on the following page represents the administrative flow from Christ, through the cell church, to the unsaved people in the community.

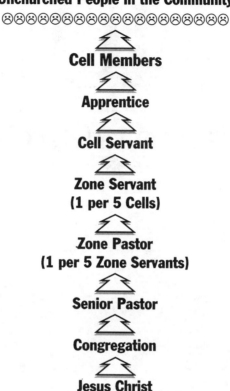

Unchurched People in the Community

Cell Members

Apprentice

Cell Servant

**Zone Servant
(1 per 5 Cells)**

**Zone Pastor
(1 per 5 Zone Servants)**

Senior Pastor

Congregation

Jesus Christ

Cell Groups

Cell Servants

Each cell group is led by a cell servant and an apprentice. The cell servant's responsibilities are as follows:

1. Attend the regular (at least monthly) cell servant planning and training sessions.

2. Lead the cell group meetings.

3. Lead the time in the Word during the cell meeting.

4. Lead and motivate the members to consistently bring new people to meetings.

5. Lead each cell group member to design and implement their personal strategy for reaching people for Christ.

6. Lead the cell group to design and implement a group strategy to assist members in reaching people for Christ.

7. Lead the cell group in setting bold yet realistic goals.

8. Model the victorious Christian life.

9. Pray daily for all cell group members and prospects.

The cell servant is the spiritual leader of the cell group. She is empowered and gifted by the Holy Spirit to lead the cell group with one or more of the servant gifts. This servant becomes the model, albeit imperfect, of the victorious Christian life and the task of reaching others for Jesus Christ. All of this is laid on the foundation of a personal relationship with Jesus Christ which is maintained and empowered through prayer. His ministry is also supported and encouraged by the zone servant and zone pastor, who are always ready to lend support and assistance as needed by the cell servant.

Apprentice
An apprentice has the following responsibilities:
1. Select the location of each cell group meeting. If meeting in homes, you should rotate the location between member's homes as much as feasible.

2. Attend the regular (at least monthly) cell servant planning and training sessions.

3. Lead the cell group meetings in the absence of the cell servant.

4. Maintain an ongoing prayer request list for the cell group. Serve as the contact person for the cell prayer chain and the prayer chain among other cells.

5. Keep all cell group attendance, membership, prospect, and ministry records.

6. Model the victorious Christian life.

7. Enlist a person each week to work with the children (in cell groups that have children). Give the person the guidesheet for the children's group for that week.

8. Arrange for discipleship of new believers through one-on-one discipleship by the cell group member who led the new believer to the Lord and discipleship through the church's new members class.

9. Lead the daughter cell group when the cell group reaches its maximum size.

The most important role of the apprentice is the coordination of the prayer life of the cell. The apprentice should purchase a notebook or notepad and keep an ongoing prayer list of the group's shared prayer requests. These can be referred to from week to week to ensure that prayer items are remembered until answered. If a critical prayer need arises during the week, members should contact the apprentice to begin a prayer chain among members. If the apprentice deems it necessary, other cell group apprentices can be contacted to extend the prayer chain to other cells.

The apprentice should maintain a list at least a month ahead of schedule for the location of each meeting and the children's worker for each meeting. The apprentice should also maintain all cell group records.

Administering a Cell Group

When a new cell group begins, the members should spend a greater portion of the first few meetings getting to know one another. Once the group has gotten acquainted, has begun to minister to needs within the group and a unity is forming, the cell should begin developing the personal and group strategies for evangelism.

Goals should be set for the new cell group in the following areas:

1. Average weekly attendance.

2. Number of new members until multiplication.

3. Date by which the cell will multiply.

4. Number of professions of faith by a designated date.

Your goals should be challenging yet realistic. The members should work together in determining the goals, since they are the ones who are responsible for reaching them.

During the first few months of a new cell, there is usually a crisis time of conflict. Different personalities may clash, values and lifestyles differ, introverts and extroverts are thrown together, and numerous other potential areas of conflict will arise. The group must learn how to work together and accept one another. Sometimes this can be done easily, but often it involves a period of conflict. This time of conflict is normal and should not be perceived as an intrusion. The cell must prayerfully, under the loving guidance of the cell servant, mature beyond the natural tendency toward self interest and become other centered and task oriented.

The goal for starting a new cell group should be the highest visible goal. The task of the group should be cell multiplication in order to counterbalance the group's natural resistance to multiplication. If expansion is not your most visible goal and the time comes for multiplying, the group may resist, stagnate, and become carnal. If the goal of multiplication is being met, all others are probably being met as well.

The primary avenue for growth should be through winning people to faith in Jesus Christ. If your growth comes from members of other churches, then you are not expanding the kingdom of God, just redistributing it.

When the average attendance reaches 15 members, the cell should multiply. A healthy cell should multiply after 6 months to 1 year. If a cell goes for more than a year without multiplying (unless the community is extremely unresponsive to the gospel, or the church has just been started and is experimenting with its evangelistic strategies), then something is wrong. The group must seek help from its zone servant and zone pastor and might even be asked to reorganize. Existing members would be redistributed to other healthy cells.

The cell group should begin planning to multiply into two cells when enrollment reaches 15 people. The zone servant, cell servant, and apprentice should prayerfully select and enlist two new leaders to become apprentices when the group multiplies. It is possible that some cells may have a leadership crisis with seemingly too many immature Christians to become servants or apprentices. It is possible to seek potential servants from other groups to move to these needy groups. But this should be rarely done. Prayerfully ask the Lord to raise up people in the group to become apprentices, while recognizing they may need additional prayer support and the direct involvement of the zone servant.

Don't let people with severe emotional problems drain the cell group of all its spiritual, emotional, and physical resources. Special cell groups may need to be formed for members that have special needs (drug abuse, chronic illnesses, depression, emotional problems, etc.). These cell groups can encourage and support severely hurting people with similar problems. Servants with special spiritual gifts need to be called out to minister to these groups.

Anyone can be a member of a cell group. The only requirement is a willingness to join. Even if the person is not a member of the church, they can join a cell group. Through the ministry of the cell group, new cell group members will be led into membership and baptism into the body.

Zone Servant

There should be a zone servant for each five cell groups. The zone servant must be an experienced and productive cell group servant. The zone servant will assist the cell group servants in their ministry and leadership. They will provide ongoing training and assist cells in designing their strategies. The zone servant will move from cell to cell and provide counsel when problems develop. Zone servants should never be responsible for more than 5 cell groups. Zone servants are under the authority of the Zone Pastor.

Zone Pastor

The zone pastor will provide pastoral leadership for up to five zone servants and their cell groups. The zone pastor is responsible for pastoral counseling, cell servant and zone servant training, personal and cell evangelism, cell ministries, coordination with the congregation, doctrinal integrity in the cells, zone goals, and other pastoral roles. The zone pastor is under the authority of the senior pastor.

Most zone pastors should be raised up from within the church. They should be men who have experienced the cell church and who understand the dynamics of cell church life. Be very careful about bringing in men as zone pastors or as senior pastor who have been trained in traditional seminaries for service in traditional churches. History has shown this to be extremely dangerous and often means the death of the cell church. Instead of bringing in outsiders, some zone servants may be asked to quit their secular jobs and enter the pastoral ministry. They may begin theological training through correspondence or by extension. Ultimately they may have to be sent to a residential seminary to complete their theological training and then return to your church.

Record Keeping

The apprentice should maintain the following records:

- *Membership*
- *Prospects*
- *Attendance Record*
- *Weekly Attendance Report*
- *Prayer Requests*
- *Prayer Chain*

When someone agrees to join as a member of your cell group, fill out the membership card. There should be two cards filled out on each member. One card should be for the church's master file, and the other should be kept by the apprentice (another may be kept by the cell servant if desired).

A prospect card should be kept for each potential cell group member. This card should be filled out on each visitor to the cell group. The person who brought the visitor should fill out the visitor card since some of the information on the card may be offensive to some non-Christian visitors. If the person visiting the cell group is not in the *oikos* of anyone in the group, the visitor should be assigned to someone in the cell group for a follow-up visit in their home. Once more information has been gathered, the visitor should be assigned to a member of the cell group. The member chosen should be the one who has the most natural *rights to relationship* with the visitor. This member, with the support of the entire cell, will take the responsibility of bringing this person or couple into their *oikos*. They should work to reach them for Christ (if unsaved) and bring them into cell membership. The quarterly attendance records are kept with the apprentice. Another small form is sent to the church to maintain a record of each cell group's weekly attendance.

The apprentice should keep a notebook or notepad during cell meetings to keep up with prayer items in the group. Acknowledging answered prayers in subsequent weeks is an important part of praise and worship. It also builds faith in God's willingness to answer prayer.

The forms on the following pages may be photocopied or modified for your church's use.

Cell Group Attendance Record
Cell Group _____

Members (Weeks)	1	2	3	4	5	6	7	8	9	10	11	12
1.												
2.												
3.												
4.												
5.												
6.												
7.												
8.												
9.												
10.												
11.												
12.												
13.												
14.												
15.												
16.												
17.												
18.												
19.												
20.												
TOTALS												

Cell Group Visitor Attendance Record
Cell Group _____

Visitors (Weeks)	1	2	3	4	5	6	7	8	9	10	11	12
1.												
2.												
3.												
4.												
5.												
6.												
7.												
8.												
9.												
10.												
11.												
12.												
13.												
14.												
15.												
16.												
17.												
18.												
19.												
20.												
TOTALS												

_____ Church

Cell Group Member

Name _____ Date _____

Address _____ Sex _____

Occupation _____ Date of Birth _____

Phone: Home _____ Business _____

Check one: _____ Married _____ Single _____ Divorced _____ Widowed

Church Member?: Yes ___ No ___

      If so, where? _____

Date of Conversion _____ Date Baptized _____

Cell Name _____ Cell Servant _____

Names and ages of children _____

_____

Training Completed:

Active Ministry Involvement:

_____ Church

Cell Group Prospect

Name_____ Date_____

From oikos of _____

    If none, assigned to: _____

Address_____ Sex_____

Occupation_____ Date of Birth_____

Phone: Home_____Business_____

Check one:_____ Married_____ Single_____Divorced_____ Widowed

Church Member?: Yes____ No____

    If so, where?_____

Christian?: Yes____ No____

    If so, Date of Conversion?:_____ Baptized?:_____

Cell Name_____ Cell Servant_____

Responsiveness to the Gospel:

Ministry Needs:

Notes:

Weekly Attendance Report

Cell Group_____ Date_____

New Members   _____

Professions of Faith   _____

Enrollment   _____

Members Present   _____

Adult Visitors Present   _____

Total Children Present   _____

                     Total Present _____

Highlights and evaluation of Meeting:

Ice Breaker

Praise

The Word

Edification

Evangelism

Prayer Chain

_____Cell Group

To initiate chain, call the Apprentice who calls each person marked with a ✮ who calls each person marked with a ✿.

Apprentice_____ ☎_____

✮Name_____ ☎_____

   ✿ Name_____ ☎_____

   ✿ Name_____ ☎_____

   ✿ Name_____ ☎_____

✮Name_____ ☎_____

   ✿ Name_____ ☎_____

   ✿ Name_____ ☎_____

   ✿ Name_____ ☎_____

✮Name_____ ☎_____

   ✿ Name_____ ☎_____

   ✿ Name_____ ☎_____

   ✿ Name_____ ☎_____

✮Name_____ ☎_____

   ✿ Name_____ ☎_____

   ✿ Name_____ ☎_____

   ✿ Name_____ ☎_____

Cell Location

List the name, phone number and date of meeting of each person hosting a cell group meeting.

Month _____

Name _____ ☎ _____ Date _____

Name _____ ☎ _____ Date _____

Name _____ ☎ _____ Date _____

Name _____ ☎ _____ Date _____

Name _____ ☎ _____ Date _____

Month _____

Name _____ ☎ _____ Date _____

Name _____ ☎ _____ Date _____

Name _____ ☎ _____ Date _____

Name _____ ☎ _____ Date _____

Name _____ ☎ _____ Date _____

Month _____

Name _____ ☎ _____ Date _____

Name _____ ☎ _____ Date _____

Name _____ ☎ _____ Date _____

Name _____ ☎ _____ Date _____

Name _____ ☎ _____ Date _____

Children's Workers

List the names, date of meeting, and phone number of each person ministering to the children during a cell group meeting.

Month _____

Name _____ ☎ _____ Date _____
Name _____ ☎ _____ Date _____
Name _____ ☎ _____ Date _____
Name _____ ☎ _____ Date _____
Name _____ ☎ _____ Date _____

Month _____

Name _____ ☎ _____ Date _____
Name _____ ☎ _____ Date _____
Name _____ ☎ _____ Date _____
Name _____ ☎ _____ Date _____
Name _____ ☎ _____ Date _____

Month _____

Name _____ ☎ _____ Date _____
Name _____ ☎ _____ Date _____
Name _____ ☎ _____ Date _____
Name _____ ☎ _____ Date _____
Name _____ ☎ _____ Date _____

Children's Guidesheet

Date:

❑ Opening Prayer

❑ Ice Breaker

❑ Songs

❑ Bible or Missions Story

❑ Sharing and Prayer

❑ Playtime or Planned Activity

❑ Refreshments

❑ Playtime

The Cell TEAM Shares

❖

What are the most important roles of the cell servant?

Why is cell multiplication so vital to a healthy cell church?

What obstacles will there be to cell multiplication?

How can internal resistance to cell multiplication be overcome?

Why are goals important for growth?

Appendix
Instructions for Prayer Walks*

❖

1. Conduct prayer walks in groups of 2 to 4 people. Wear jogging or walking clothes so as not to create suspicion by the neighbors.

2. Before you start your walk, pray together in a private place such as one of your homes:
   - Prepare yourselves by coming into the presence of God with a time of praise to God.
   - Confess all known sin to God and one another.
   - Claim that you are protected by the full armor of God. (Gird your loins with truth, put on the breastplate of righteousness, the helmet of salvation, shod your feet with the preparation of the gospel of peace, take up the shield of faith and the sword of the Spirit.)
   - Pray for the filling of the Holy Spirit, for discernment and wisdom in whom, how and what to pray for as you walk.
   - Pray for protection for yourselves as you walk, for your family members, and your homes.

3. Go together to the starting point of your prayer walk and:
   - Claim the streets you will walk for Christ.
   - Ask the Lord to:
     - pour out the Holy Spirit upon them,

- convict them of their sin,
- lead them to repentance,
- bring circumstances and events into their lives to draw them to Christ, and
- bring someone into their lives to lead them to Christ.

4. Start walkin;, do not walk fast, but keep moving. Examine each house. Look for clues to a family's lifestyle and priorities.

5. Pray for each house or establishment.
   - Claim each home for Jesus Christ.
   - Pray for the salvation of each household.
   - Ask the Lord to rebuke the work of Satan against them, and that the blinding of the evil one would be removed.
   - Ask the Lord Jesus to remove any footholds (or strongholds) of the evil one in the lives of household members as you feel led of the Spirit.
   - Pray that their eyes may be opened to the truth, and that they would be responsive to the ministry of the body of Christ (or a specific strategy you are planning to use).
   - Pray for a man or woman of peace that the Lord would prepare to respond to your ministry and be used to penetrate the neighborhood with the gospel.

6. If you experience a strange or evil feeling, make a note of the location, command the evil one to leave your presence, and move on. Report this to your leadership, and corporately seek the Lord's guidance as to what the problem is and how to proceed. A prayer walk team should not directly confront centers of witchcraft, animistic worship, religious shrines or cults, new age, or blatant sexual perversion.

7. Close in a time of praise to God for what He has done and will do. Praise Him for His victory upon the cross, the defeat of the evil one, and the victory He will bring in your community.

*If there is habitual sin in your life or someone you are unwilling to forgive, resolve these matters before participating in prayer walks. Tools like the *Bondage Breaker* by Neal T. Anderson are helpful in dealing with these issues.